ENTANGLEMENTS

A Novel Written by Debra Chappelle-Polk

A POWER COUPLE'S LAVISH LIFESTYLE IS ENTANGLED
IN SECRET DESIRES, FORBIDDEN LOVE AND
PLEASURES LEADING TO DEADLY CONSEQUENCES.

DEBRA CHAPPELLE-POLK

authorHOUSE

AuthorHouse™
1663 Liberty Drive
Bloomington, IN 47403
www.authorhouse.com
Phone: 833-262-8899

Published by AuthorHouse 03/17/2022

ISBN: 978-1-6655-2062-1 (sc)
ISBN: 978-1-6655-2064-5 (hc)
ISBN: 978-1-6655-2063-8 (e)

Library of Congress Control Number: 2021913713

Print information available on the last page.

This book is printed on acid-free paper.

CHAPTER 1

Las Vegas – June 1985

It was like a scene from a Hollywood movie. In fact, a screenwriter could not have scripted it better.

Renee Elise was walking toward the hotel lobby elevator. She was carrying a small make-up kit full of new products and her tote bag was loaded with brochures and pamphlets. Her feet were killing her. Why hadn't she worn sneakers instead of these cute, but uncomfortable sandals? She got to the elevator and dug into the inner pocket of her tote bag for her room key card. It wasn't there. She tilted the bag to one side and felt the key card which had fallen to the bottom of the bag. As she grabbed the key card, it fell from her hand onto the carpeted floor.

"Darn it!" Renee dropped her tote bag, and the brochures spilled out onto the floor.

Kenny Wallace stepped off the elevator. He saw Renee and a key card on the floor. They both reached down at the same time to pick it up. Their eyes locked, and they narrowly avoided head-butting each other.

"Yours?" Kenny smiled and picked up the key card.

"Yes. Thank you." She took the key card from him and started shoving the brochures into her bag.

"Here, let me help you." He cautiously bent down to help her.

"Thanks, I didn't realize how much stuff I was carrying."

"Yeah, who knew paper could be so heavy?" Kenny said attempting to be funny.

"Yeah, who knew? Renee pushed the elevator button. "Thanks again."

My pleasure. Miss...?

"Elise, Renee Elise."

"It's a pleasure to meet you. I'm Kenny Wallace."

"Nice to meet you, Mr. Wallace."

"Kenny. My father's Mr. Wallace." He saw the look on Renee's face.

"Okay, it's old and corny." He shrugged.

Renee smiled. "Yes, it is."

"I have some new material I can share with you over lunch."

"I bet you do, but I have lunch plans." She looked him up and down.

He was standing in front of a beautiful woman and he wasn't about to let her get away. "How about dinner? The hotel's famous for its restaurants." He smiled.

Renee was impressed by Kenny's persistence. "Alright, dinner."

"Great. I'll make reservations. Any preferences?"

"Surprise me."

"Hey, I like the way you think. I'll meet you at 7 by the rain forest waterfall."

"The rain forest waterfall at 7. See you then." She stepped into the elevator.

Renee got to her room, kicked off her sandals and rubbed her aching toes. She took the brochures out of her tote and made a keep pile and a toss pile. Her 'lunch plans' were to order room service and review her notes from the seminar on developing websites.

Renee was elated to be representing the LTH brand at

the beauty supply convention in Las Vegas. The convention had been informative. She was there to learn, and she had gotten what she came for. She had met people from all over the country knowledgeable in every aspect of the beauty supply and products industry. The convention organizers had also arranged a mini-tour of the City and she had seen some of the sites Vegas was famous for. At 22, she already had a bucket list; a trip to Vegas being high on the list. Having dinner with a handsome guy she bumped into front of the elevator wasn't on her bucket list, but what the hay.

She finished her lunch and review. After showering, she looked over her Vegas wardrobe, trying to decide what to wear to dinner. She settled on a cream-colored halter dress and bronze metallic sandals. Renee was slim and trim. The dress was subtly sexy, and the color complimented her cocoa brown skin tone. She let her long reddish-brown hair flow freely and touched up her makeup. She checked the time: 7:15 on the dot. She took one last glance in the mirror, gave herself a thumbs up and was out the door.

Kenny had been standing in front of the rain forest waterfall since 6:45. He was early not because he was anxious, but because he wanted to watch Renee as she walked toward him. He knew she was pretty, but he hadn't seen the full package. He had a feeling she wouldn't disappoint. He was right.

Kenny had made reservations at one of the hotel's rooftop restaurants. The hostess escorted them to a booth with a panoramic view of the city.

Kenny pulled out a chair for Renee.

"You look great." Kenny said.

"Thanks."

"Good evening. I'm Phil and I'll be your server tonight." He smiled, as he placed menus on the table. "Can I start you guys off with something to drink?"

"What would you like?" Kenny asked Renee.

"Rum and coke."

"Two rum and cokes."

"Coming right up. In the meantime, check out the menu. Everything is good, but I highly recommend the red snapper. It's delish." Phil smiled again.

"Thanks, Phil." Kenny said.

"Have you been here before?" Renee asked.

"Vegas or the restaurant?"

"Both."

"Yes, and yes. I've been to Vegas a few times and I've always enjoyed the food here. What about you? Have you been to Vegas before?

"Nope. This is my first time. I'm here for the Beauty Suppliers and Distributors' annual convention."

Kenny nodded. "Vegas is the convention capital of the world. I'm here for the investors' convention."

Phil returned with their drinks. "Ready to order?"

Renee was still looking at the menu. "I can't decide between the snapper and the grilled chicken."

"The snapper's good. You should try it." Kenny suggested.

"I did ask you to surprise me. Okay, I'll have the snapper."

Over dinner, Renee told Kenny she sold beauty supplies and products for a hair care company.

"I'm especially interested in new marketing strategies to get your brand out there. I'm going to take a more advanced computer class when I get home."

"And where's home?"

"Brooklyn, New York." Renee answered.

"Hey, we're neighbors. I live in the Village."

"We're hardly neighbors, but we do live in the same state."

"Same city." Kenny corrected.

"Okay, same city." She smiled. "So, how was your investors' convention?"

"Boring as usual. A lot of numbers, graphs and statistics. The formal sessions ended this afternoon. Tonight's the three Bs."

"The three Bs?"

"Booze, boobs and babes. It's Atlas' reward for our hard work."

The phrase what happens in Vegas, stays in Vegas popped into Renee's head.

"So why aren't you at the three Bs?"

"Been there, done that. Too much testosterone and too many tequila shots."

"Really, you passed on booze, boobs, what was the third B?"

"Babes."

"Babes. Really, you passed on that?" Renee was shaking her head.

"Yes, I did. Plus, I'm having dinner with you." Kenny smiled.

Kenny was glad he passed on the 3Bs. He much preferred having dinner with Renee. She was beautiful and the more she talked, the more mesmerizing she became.

Phil reappeared. "Dessert?

They both declined, but Kenny didn't want the evening to end.

"Harold's is a great club not far from here with a terrific band. We can have a nightcap."

Renee looked at her watch.

"Come on, it's early. Just one nightcap and if you don't like the music, we can leave."

"Alright. One nightcap."

Harold's wasn't far from the hotel. Renee was glad about that in the event she decided to dump Kenny and had to find her way back to the hotel.

Harold's was surprisingly quiet for a Vegas nightclub. They found a table and Kenny ordered two rum and cokes. A three-piece band was playing a medley of songs from the 80s.

Renee looked around the club.

Kenny was watching her. "Is this okay?" He asked.

"Yes." Harold's reminded her of Darling's.

"You sure?" Her body language suggested otherwise.

"It reminds me of the club where my father's band plays."

"Your father has his own band. That's pretty cool." Kenny was genuinely impressed.

"My father plays the sax, and my brother plays the drums." She didn't tell him that Darling's was owned by the woman her father left her mother for.

"I haven't heard that song in a while." Renee said. "Brings back memories."

"It's one of my favorites, too. They don't make them like anymore." Kenny wondered if her memories were good ones.

"I'd like to see you when we get back to the City. Here's my card."

She read the card. Kenny Wallace Investment & Accounting Firm.

"You own an investment company?

"Firm. Investment Firm."

"You invest other peoples' money and make them a lot of money?"

Kenny smiled. He was amused by her description of what he does.

"Pretty much, although there are some risks involved."

"How long have you been making people money?"

"I started my own firm a few years ago. Before that, I was Atlas' Investments first token."

"Token as in the only black person with a desk and who doesn't clean the toilets?" She asked.

"Yep."

"How did that work out?"

"It was a challenge. The *good-ole-boy* culture was still alive and kicking. Not to mention that some of my colleagues were dyed-in-the wool racists who thought I should have been shining their shoes, and I'm sure they told nigger jokes when I wasn't around."

"How did you deal with it?"

"I kept my cool. My motto: never let 'em see you sweat."

"Still, it must have been difficult. I hoped they paid you the same as your white colleagues. 'Tokens' generally get paid less for doing the same job."

"True. They think you should be happy they hired you. That's your compensation. However, I brought in a lot of business and made the firm a lot of money, which was really what it was all about. I made as much, sometimes more, than my white counterparts. I bought my first condo and opened my own firm." He ran down his history.

She heard the boasting. "I guess nothing beats a try but failure."

"I don't fail." Kenny stated with confidence. "Have you ever thought about starting your own business? The beauty supply business is competitive, but profitable with the right management."

"Actually, I have. My mother was the neighborhood hairdresser. She set up a 'beauty salon' in the living room of our Bronx apartment. She *cooked up* mixtures in our kitchen that increased hair growth using natural ingredients. She was inspired by Madame CJ Walker, whose line of hair care products for Black women had made her the first Black female self-made millionaire in the late 1890s."

"I'm familiar with Madam CJ's story. Is your mother still 'cooking up' her mixtures?"

"Sadly, no. She died a few years ago."

"Sorry."

"Yeah, so am I." Renee said reflectively, "But she left me the 'recipe'."

"If it works, you might have yourself a product and a company."

"Oh, it works. I know lots of ladies who swear by it." Renee also had a few bottles of the mixture, but more importantly, she knew what was in it. Problem is she didn't have start-up money.

"I might be able to help." It was if he had read her mind.

"Really? It's not too small time?"

"Not at all. I've helped a lot of start-ups. Matter of fact, I've turned a lot of small businesses into big businesses. I know how hard it is for young entrepreneurs to get funding."

Renee was excited. She had thought about starting her own hair care line for a long time. It might be worth getting to know this guy if he can do what he says he can.

She smiled and handed him her card.

"LT Hair? Is that the name of the company you work for?"

"Yes, it is. The LT stands for Lisa Taylor, the owner."

"How long have you worked for Lisa Taylor?"

"For a while." She answered without being specific.

"Well, that could change very soon." Kenny smiled and raised his glass. 'To Renee's Hair.'

"Renee's Hair Care. I like that." She raised her glass.

"You're not married, are you?"

Renee frowned. Her mind flashed to Bernard Burkes, her drug-dealing ex-fiancé about whom she still had nightmares.

"Sore subject?"

"I'm not married."

"Neither am I."

Renee looked at her watch. "Wow, it's past midnight and I still need to pack."

"Yeah, me too. I'm on the Delta redeye to JFK."

"I'm flying Delta into JFK also, but on a later flight."

They walked back to the hotel. They were standing in front of the same elevator where they almost bumped heads earlier. They looked at each other and laughed at the irony.

"Here, we are again." Renee said.

"Ladies first. What floor?"

"Seventeen."

"I'm on forty-two." Kenny pushed the button for both floors.

"Ooh, the penthouse." Renee chuckled.

The elevator reached the 17th floor and Kenny held the door as Renee was getting off. "I had a wonderful evening. Have a safe flight. I'll call you."

"Goodnight." Renee got off the elevator.

Kenny went to his room. He took a shower and was sitting on the side of his king-size bed. He hadn't plan to come to the convention this year. He figured it would be the same old stuff packaged in a new shiny wrapper. The 3Bs was old, as were the strippers. Meeting Renee Elise, however, had made the trip worthwhile. She was young and fresh. He guessed she was about 5'6 and 115 pounds, give or take. He didn't ask her how old she was, but she looked to be around 22, perhaps younger, which was a definite plus in his book. Her willingness to try new things, (*"surprise me"*) was also a plus. She seemed to be a real go-getter. He watched as her face lit up when he suggested she start her own beauty products line. When he came up with the name Renee's Hair Care, he was certain he had sealed the deal and she would be in his bed right about now. Not tonight, Kenny. However, he wasn't disappointed. He knew that day would come when she would be. He poured himself a drink and sat out on the balcony watching the Vegas lights. He started drawing up a business plan for Renee's Hair.

Kenny landed at New York's JFK Airport and he checked the arrivals board. There was a flight from Vegas landing at 2 o'clock. Since it was the only one, he figured it was Renee's flight. He thought about waiting, however, upon second thought, he realized she might misinterpret his eagerness and decided against it.

Renee settled into her seat on the plane which was at the end of cabin near the bathroom. She was going ask for her seat to be changed, until she realized she had the entire back row to herself. She stretched out, making herself comfortable. She put the headphones on and found smooth jazz channel.

The trip had been good. She learned a lot and her encounter

with Kenny Wallace had been interesting. Experience had taught her that men were two-legged dogs who pissed on everything and couldn't be trusted, but he seemed different.

Renee mentally critiqued Kenny. Handsome, light-skin Black man came to mind. Although he hadn't disclosed his age, she figured he was around 35. He looked to be about 6 feet tall and in good shape. It would not have surprised her if he had a membership at an expensive fitness club in Manhattan. After all, he owned a condo in the Village and an investment firm. He was a bit full of himself, but maybe he had to be to succeed in the investment world.

'*Renee's Hair Care.*' She loved the name and if he could make that happen, she would do whatever was necessary.

When her plane landed, Lisa Taylor was waiting at the Delta terminal curbside passenger pick up area. Renee quickly threw her bag in the backseat and jumped in the car. On the drive home, Renee gave Lisa a detailed report of the events in Vegas.

Her detailed report omitted Kenny Wallace.

Kenny called Renee later that day and got her voicemail. He left a short message saying he hoped had she arrived home safely and asked her to give him a call. She didn't.

They do, however, talk the following day. Her flight home had been smooth, and the plane landed on time. They agreed to meet for drinks the following evening.

For the next several months, Kenny wined and dined Renee at five-star restaurants in Manhattan, bistros in Brooklyn and seafood eateries on City Island in the Bronx.

Kenny talked a lot about his himself. He was Kenneth and

Marie Wallace's only child. He grew up in a 3-bedroom home in an affluent neighborhood on Long Island. His father, Kenneth Wallace, Sr. had been a civil engineer. His mother had been a nurse. Both were now retired and were talented singers. The chemistry between his parents was apparent from day one. The difference between them was also apparent. *'My father's onyx and my mother's lily white. I'm a homogeneous blend.'*

Kenny graduated *Suma Cum Laude* from Howard University with a degree in accounting and business administration. He started his career at Atlas Investment and within a year, was earning well over 6 figures.

Kenny was borderline obnoxious, but charming. He intuitively knew just when to stop talking about himself.

Renee was impressed and intimated by Kenny's pedigree. Her childhood hadn't been nearly as idyllic as Kenny's. She grew up in a Bronx apartment, not a house on Long Island. After she graduated from high school, she enrolled in a community college but had to drop out after her mother got sick. The 'chemistry' (Kenny's word) between her parents was toxic. Her father had cheated on her mother. He and her brother were now living with her father's mistress.

They were at a Karaoke bar club in Harlem. Kenny took mike, sang and won first prize: half-priced Tequila shots on his next visit.

"You're pretty good. I guess you get it from your dad."

"I'm not nearly as good, but thanks. Dad would be proud."

"I have something to show you." He handed her a manila envelope.

Renee opened the envelope. "It's the business plan for Renee's Hair Care."

Kenny nodded. "Yes, it is."

He had kept his word.

"It's a sound plan, if I do say so myself."

She flipped to the last page, which listed the start-up costs.

"Don't worry about the start-up costs. I'll take care of that. All I need from you right now is a sample of the product for the chemist to test."

"Oh, it works."

"I'm not doubting you, but it still needs to be tested for quality assurance purposes and to make sure it's in compliance with industry regulations for commercial use."

"And what else do you want from me?" Renee asked.

"Nothing?"

"Nothing? Eyebrow raised.

"Okay, maybe not nothing. We'll negotiate after the business takes off and trust me, it will." He winked and smiled.

Renee's decided to go for it. The next day, she gave Kenny a bottle of the hair growth mixture. Within a month, Kenny had secured a chemist and testing lab. The chemist certified the formula was safe and met industry standards for commercial use. Renee was elated. All she needed was a patent. Kenny took care of that as well.

They celebrated Renee's new business, *Renee's Hair Care*, with a home-cooked dinner at Kenny's apartment. It was the first time they slept together. Kenny was great in the kitchen but not so great in the bedroom.

Renee wasn't critical of his performance. Irrationally, she attributed Kenny's lackluster performance to the fact *she* hadn't had sex with man in years and was nervous. Neither had anything to do with Kenny's sexual performance.

Kenny lost his virginity when he was 16. The girl was 14. As he got older, his sexual partners got younger. Women his age did nothing for him. Try as he might, and he tried a lot, *nada*. He then used an escort service that specialized in providing women who looked like teenage girls. It worked, until it didn't. He then resorted to pornography. He convinced himself he was only watching for tutorial purposes.

Even though Renee was 22 and older than he would have liked, Kenny found her sexually appealing. He chalked up his performance (or lack thereof) to him having too much to drink. He convinced himself the sex would get better, and that Renee would 'cure' him of his proclivities.

Renee had been seeing Kenny for almost six months, but she still hadn't told Lisa about Kenny or about Renee's Hair Care. Lisa had noticed Renee was aloof, almost secretive, and suspected something was going on. Her suspicions were confirmed when she found the business plan for Renee's Hair Care.

Renee returned home after a night out with Kenny. Lisa was sitting on the sofa waiting for her. An open bottle of wine was on the table. A manila envelope was also on the table.

"Hey, you didn't have to wait up for me. I told you I'd be late." Renee said in what she hoped was a calm voice.

"Where you been?"

"What?"

"Oh, we're gonna to play the *"what?"* game. I asked you where you've been?" Her words were slightly slurred.

"Are you drunk?" Renee sat down and poured herself a drink.

"Don't even try it. I'm not drunk and don't try to change the subject. I know you."

"Okay, since you know me so well, then you know where I've been." Renee swallowed her drink and stood up.

"Do you think I'm stupid?" Lisa grabbed Renee and tried to pull her down onto the sofa.

"Don't make me hurt you, Lisa." Renee bent Lisa's arm backward.

"Ow! that hurt." Lisa rubbed her arm.

"I'm sorry. But you know how I get when I feel threatened."

"I found this." Lisa pushed the manila envelope toward Renee.

Renee opened the envelope even though she already knew what was in it. "I was going to talk to you about this."

"So, talk."

"Okay, here's the deal. It's a business plan."

"Duh. *Renee's Hair Care.*"

"I met this guy named Kenny Wallace in Vegas who owns an investment firm. We started talking and I told him I sold beauty and hair care products. He said he might be interested in investing. Like I said, he's an investor."

"Are you sleeping with him?"

"What?"

"Oh, so we're still playing the *'what'* game?"

"Kenny's an investor. Investor's, invest." She was not ready for this conversation.

"Are you sleeping with him?" Lisa enunciated each word.

"Yes."

"Correct me if I'm wrong: you haven't slept with a man a while. Am I right?

"You're right."

"So, how was it after all this time?"

Renee sighed. "Terrible."

"Great." They both started laughing.

"Is it serious?" Lisa was dreading Renee's response, but she needed to know.

"At first, I thought it was. Sorry."

"So, that's means it's not serious?" Lisa asked.

"I don't know. I mean he's really nice, rich as hell and wasn't trying to jump my bones. Then when he tried, he couldn't." Renee sighed again.

Lisa was practically howling. "Big money, little wing-ding."

Renee was laughing too. "No, that's not it. I mean it's big enough, but he doesn't......" she stopped abruptly, thinking about the problem for the first time.

"Okay, so what are you going to do?" Lisa asked.

"Do about what? His wing-ding?

"Yeah, if you *really* want it, but I'm talking about the investment part. You said he's got money. If he can get us to where we want to go, play the game. I'll always be here to take care of Missy."

"Well," Renee slipped off her panties and laid flat on her back on the sofa. "Missy's waiting."

CHAPTER 2

Renee Elise grew up in a large six-room apartment on the Grand Concourse in the Bronx. From the 1920s to the 1940s, the Grand Concourse was home to middle-class Jewish and Italian American families. Over the decades, the Grand Concourse underwent demographic and economic changes, resulting in the "white flight." Large spacious apartments, some with two bathrooms and maids' quarters, were now available to working-class Black families.

Her father, Alvin Elise was an elevator mechanic who played a mean saxophone on weekends at various night spots.

Her mother, Karen, was a school-crossing guard and the neighborhood hairdresser. Karen began doing hair in the dining room where two or three friends would stop by for a press and curl. They started bringing their daughters for a wash and set, which morphed into perms, which morphed into weaves. To accommodate her growing clientele, her mother converted one of the bedrooms into a hair salon. Every Saturday, neighborhood women lined up outside the Karen's door.

Renee was a senior in high school and her brother Robert was a freshman at a community college. The Elise siblings saw an opportunity to advance the family business and started selling food to the customers as they waited to have their hair done. Fried hair and fried chicken. To say the customers *ate it up* was an understatement. Renee and Robert also started scouting out storefronts where they could open a real beauty salon.

Alvin played his horn at Darling's, a bar owned by Darlene

Brown, on Friday and Saturday nights, which usually turned into Sunday mornings. Alvin was a handsome, sexy man who knew how to blow a horn. The women were crazy about him. The fact that he was married in some ways made him even more attractive.

Everyone (except Karen) knew that Darlene and Alvin were messing around. Darlene had a great place to work and play. There was always plenty of liquor to drink and coke to sniff.

When the space next to Darling's became vacant, Darlene had an opportunity to expand her club. The offer was reasonable, but she would still need a partner. She asked Alvin to be her partner. Alvin agreed without talking to Karen about it.

Karen learned of Alvin's new business when she discovered he had withdrawn a substantial amount from their bank account. She confronted Alvin about the withdrawal. Alvin was tired and hungover. He told Karen he wasn't in the mood for her bitching. Karen told Alvin she wasn't in the mood for his bullshit. She suspected he was cheating on her, but the missing money was the last straw. They had a loud, profanity-laced argument, most of which Renee and her brother Robert overheard. Alvin left. Robert was upset when his father moved out, and he blamed his mother. After a ferocious argument, Robert went to live with his father and Darlene.

Shortly thereafter, Karen was diagnosed with breast cancer and was unable to work. The money from the hair business was being rapidly depleted. To help pay the rent, Renee got a job selling hair care products for LTH (Lisa Taylor Hair).

Renee told her brother Robert about their mother's cancer and the state of their finances. Robert told his father. Both were sympathetic and gave Renee *a few dollars*, to help with the rent when they could, which wasn't often.

Karen Elise lost her battle with breast cancer a year later. Alvin attended his wife's funeral and brought his girlfriend Darlene. Renee was irate. As Alvin approached his late wife's coffin, Renee erupted and bolted from her seat with her arms flailing, screaming at her father. She was so overcome with grief and anger she nearly fainted. Family members rushed to Renee to prevent her from falling.

Renee was struggling to pay the rent and was a month away from eviction. Her father and brother suggested she find an apartment she could afford.

Renee's boyfriend, Bernard (BernieB) Burkes, had a solution. He had a friend who was looking for a place. He suggested that Renee sublet the apartment to his friend and move in with him. He also told her he wanted to marry her. The money from the sublet would pay for their wedding and honeymoon.

Renee thought her prayers had been answered: she was getting married and would live happily ever after with her new husband.

She moved in with Bernard Burkes, but they never got married. BernieB was a drug dealer. His friend moved into Renee's apartment and sold drugs from the apartment.

Renee learned of her boyfriend's deception, when a woman who lived in the same building told her about the drugs being sold from her apartment. Renee could not believe what she was hearing and said she was going to call the police. The neighbor told Renee she was going to get herself killed if she did. *"Girl, are you crazy? Those guys don't be playing. They will shoot you in the head, chop up your body and throw your bones in a landfill.*"

Renee didn't call the cops. Instead, she rushed home to tell Bernard. BernieB and two of his friends were watching a basketball game. Renee knew from experience that it was useless to try to have a conversation with him while he was watching a game. By halftime, however, she could no longer contain herself. She called him into the bedroom and told him what was going on in her apartment, stupidly assuming he didn't already know what was going on. She was wrong. BernieB was the ringleader. He threw Renee up against the wall. He squeezed his hands around her throat and threatened to kill her if she even thought about going to the police. He then threw on the bed and raped her. Then his two friends raped her as he watched. He told her he and his friends were going out and she'd better be gone by the time they got back.

Renee was dazed and in pain. She managed to throw some of her things in a bag and left the apartment. She didn't know where to go or who to call.

She called Lisa Taylor and said she had been raped. Lisa told Renee to take a cab to her apartment in Brooklyn. Lisa was downstairs when the cab pulled up to her door. She paid the fare, picked up Renee's bag and took her to her apartment.

The next day, Renee related all the horrid details to Lisa. She was traumatized but refused to go to the police. Lisa despised what had happened to Renee but understood why she didn't want to go to the police.

Lisa Taylor ran her business (LTH) which was a line of facial and hair care products for women from her home. Renee had been living and working from Lisa's apartment for about six months. Renee knew the product line and sales had increased by nearly 30 percent. With her commissions increasing, Renee told Lisa she was going to look for a place of her own. Lisa told her it really wasn't necessary. In fact, she was hoping she'd move in permanently. Renee was a bit gun shy after the last offer to move in with someone had gone horribly wrong. Lisa understood and told Renee to take her time.

One bright sunny morning in July, Lisa packed lunch, two bathing suits and drove to the beach. They sunbathed, swam in the ocean, and ate hero sandwiches. When they got home, Renee said she was going to take a shower. Lisa kissed her lips and asked if it would be alright if she joined her. Renee nodded and smiled. After they showered together, Lisa invited Renee to her bed. Renee experienced the most exquisite orgasm she had ever had.

CHAPTER 3

Kenny Wallace opened Kenny Wallace Investment & Accounting Firm in the early 80s. Because it was a Black-owned investment firm, it generated a lot of media buzz and curiosity. Major news organizations and magazines wanted to interview Kenny, who had been dubbed The Black Financial Wizard. Kenny had mixed feelings about his new moniker, but decided he needed to get his name out there, and this was free advertisement. He granted interviews and his picture was *all over the place*. The free publicity paid off and within a few years the firm was a multi-million-dollar investment firm.

Kenny Wallace was falling in love with Renee, and from his perspective, Renee was falling in love with him. He was wrong. Renee genuinely enjoyed being with him, but it wasn't love.

Renee and Lisa were in love. However, they both agreed it was in their best interest that Renee continue to see Kenny. Although it was business, neither were thrilled with the arrangement, especially Renee. Sex with Kenny was a hit or miss sort of situation, with more misses than hits. Renee closed her eyes, moaned and faked orgasms.

With Kenny's help, Renee's Hair Care products were being sold in drugstores around the city. Renee thought LTH would be a good distributor as well. Kenny was ambivalent. Nonetheless, he agreed to a meeting with Lisa Taylor, and drew up a limited agreement on the oft chance Renee was right. The three met for lunch. It was summer and Kenny reserved an outside patio table at a posh restaurant in midtown Manhattan.

Kenny and Renee were sitting at their table when Lisa

arrived. Kenny wasn't sure what he expected. Renee had only told him that Lisa was about 15 years older than she was and a good businesswoman. He watched as she approached their table. She was a pretty, petite dark-skinned woman, stylishly attired. Kenny noticed the diamond stud earrings. From the contours of her body, it was evident she worked out and she certainly didn't look 15 years older than Renee. The only off-putting thing about Lisa Taylor was her clean-shaven head. It seemed a bit peculiar to Kenny that a woman who sold hair products didn't have any.

She greeted Renee with a kiss on her cheek.

"Lisa, this is Kenny Wallace"

"It's a pleasure to meet you, Ms. Taylor."

Lisa smiled. "The pleasure is all mine, Mr. Wallace."

"Kenny. Please call me Kenny. Mr. Wallace is my father."

"So, Kenny, I understand you're an investor." She smiled again. "And as I'm sure Renee has already told you, I'm looking to take LT Hair to the next level, which is why I agreed to take this meeting."

Kenny listened as Lisa talked about her experience in the beauty and hair industry. He was impressed and convinced an arrangement with LTH would be a good thing. They signed the agreement and Kenny ordered a bottle of champagne. The car Lisa had ordered to take her home arrived. She shook hands with Kenny and kissed Renee on the cheek, promising to call her later.

Kenny took Renee shopping to celebrate. They were near the diamond district and stopped in a store, where the owner greeted Kenny by name. He invited them to his office to look at some pieces he had recently acquired. Renee listened as the

24

owner described the carat weight and settings of the various rings. Kenny suggested she try on some of the rings. She selected a 2-carat diamond solitaire with a yellow gold band. She held up her ring finger admiring the ring.

"What do you think?" She asked.

Kenny frowned. "It's okay, but we can do better. Try something else, babe."

Renee tried on six rings, all of which received the *we-can-do-better frown.*

The 7th *time was the charm:* she tried on a pear-shaped 5-carat diamond with sapphires. It fit her finger perfectly and looked good on her hand.

"Now, that's what I'm talking 'bout!"

Kenny had already decided that Renee would be his wife. Although the owner's office wasn't the opulent setting he had envisioned, he nonetheless got down on one knee and proposed. Despite the fact she had been trying on engagement rings, Renee was totally shocked, and it showed on her face. She started to cry. Kenny didn't know what to think. Were these good tears or bad tears? The wheels in Renee's head were spinning. As Kenny was about to stand up, Renee bent down. Once again, they narrowly avoided butting heads. They laughed.

"So, Renee Elise, will you marry me?"

"Yes, Kenny Wallace I will marry you."

The jeweler, who had been standing near the door popped open a bottle of champagne. "Mazel tov!"

When they got to Kenny's apartment, he told her he had ordered dinner and asked her to spend the night. He had already planned how their lives would be moving forward from the engagement party to the wedding, and of course, the honeymoon.

"I figured we'd do the engagement party at the Four Seasons. I'll check what's available. We can do the wedding at the Waldorf. I'm not much of a church guy, but if you'd like a church wedding, I'll make some calls. By the way, would you prefer a spring or summer wedding?" Kenny spit all this out like he was planning an event for his firm. He hadn't noticed that Renee hadn't said anything.

"I figured I'd have to foot the whole bill, but no big deal. And I think you should ask your dad to walk you down the aisle.

"No." Renee's head was still spinning, but that got her attention.

"You know what a planner I am. What's the problem?"

She hadn't *planned* on any of this. That was the problem. Plus, he knew how she felt about her father. How dare he?

"Once again, in typical Kenny Wallace fashion, you've planned everything. Next, you'll be *planning* what dress I'm wearing and my underwear underneath."

Kenny was taken aback by Renee's tone.

"I'm sorry. I thought you'd be happy." Kenny sounded like a little boy apologizing to his mother.

Renee softened her voice. She almost felt sorry for him. "I am happy, Kenny, but this is such a surprise. I need time to digest all of it." She gently kissed his lips. "I've already made plans for the weekend. Why don't we talk more about everything on Monday?"

"Oh, okay, but I have an out- of- town business meeting on Monday and won't be back until later in the week. We can talk then and finalize everything." Kenny relaxed, but he had expected Renee to be excited that he had proposed.

Renee breathed what she hoped was a silent sigh of relief and practically ran home to Lisa.

Lisa's damp workout shorts and sports bra were on the floor outside the bathroom. Renee heard the shower running. She stripped and jumped in. Lisa was momentarily startled. She took one look at Renee's face and immediately knew what she needed. They lathered each other up with a lavender and honeysuckle scented body wash (a new LTH product), then rinsed off. Lisa dried Renee's body with a huge towel and led her to the bedroom. That's when Lisa noticed Renee's ring.

"What the fuck is that?!" Lisa held up Renee's hand. "Oh no, don't tell me the man with the little wing-ding proposed?"

"Yes."

"Shut the front door! Take it off."

"What?"

"Take it off. I want to try it on."

Renee took off the ring and slipped her ring onto Lisa's finger. "Lisa Taylor, will you marry me?"

"Yes, Renee Elise, I'll marry you." Lisa nodded and kissed her.

There was a sadness to her voice. They love each other, but it was a forbidden love, and to some, an abomination. Tears welled up in Lisa's eyes.

"*Da....mn*, how much did this puppy set him back?" She twirled the ring around her finger. Her composure was back intact.

"I didn't ask, but trust me, I'm sure he'll tell me. He's probably already had it appraised and insured."

"So, what you gonna do? You planning to be Mrs. Little Wing-Ding?" Lisa started to laugh but, stopped abruptly when she looked at Renee's face. "What's wrong? Talk to me."

"I don't know. I've ---- *we've* invested a lot and the company's doing better than either one of us ever imagined, mostly due to Kenny and don't think he doesn't know it. If I don't marry him, he might pull the plug on Renee's Hair Care."

"I don't think he'd pull the plug, but I do think he'd find a way to gain complete ownership. Kenny's an investor and he invests. If he didn't think Renee's Hair Care was a good investment, he wouldn't have invested and don't forget, he's made more than a few coins with Renee's Hair Care."

"Are you saying he's marrying me because it's a good investment?"

"No. Well, not exactly." Lisa said.

"Then what exactly? Come on, Lisa, you're not good at holding your tongue."

"I'm not saying he doesn't love you. He probably does. I mean, what's not to love? You're attractive, smart and got a great bod, to which I can attest." Lisa pinched her nipple.

"This is serious, Lisa." She pushed her hand away.

"Okay, okay. I know it's serious. Marry him. Let him take Renee's Hair Care to the 5-million-dollar sales zone. Just make sure you retain all licensing and proprietary rights. If he's anything like you say he is, he'll probably want you to sign a prenup. In the meantime, I'll do a background check."

"As in private detective?" Renee laughed.

"If necessary. Everybody's got something in their proverbial closet, and men with wing-ding performance issues always overcompensate. I'm sure there's something there. It'll be your insurance policy if he gets shitty when you divorce him." Lisa stated with confidence, as if she already knew something.

"Divorce? You have to be married before you can get a divorce. And what makes you so sure I said yes?

"Because you're wearing the ring."

CHAPTER 4

The Kenny and Renee Wallace wedding was extravagant and expensive. Kenny invited over 100 guests, most of whom were business contacts rather than friends, but it didn't matter. He was planning to write off most of the wedding expenses anyway. His parents and grandparents were happy. They didn't know much about their daughter-in-law other than she was pretty and the owner of Renee's Hair Care, a very successful hair care business.

They honeymooned in Rome and returned to Kenny's latest acquisition: a new penthouse condo in the Village.

Kenny and Renee worked long hours. Kenny was busy recruiting new investors and Renee was in the lab concocting new products. She managed to visit Lisa at least once or twice a week.

Renee was at Lisa's house having lunch when she started to feel ill and threw up her guts. Lisa put a damp cloth on her forehead and told her she was pregnant. Renee threw up again.

Renee gave birth to Erika Marie Wallace on June 27, 1992. She also had her tubes tied.

Though Erika's mother was gorgeous, and her father was a handsome geek, Erika was decidedly plain and at age 3, was still non-verbal. Renee and Kenny were worried. They had Erika evaluated by medical specialists who told them to be patient, lots of children had delayed speech. The specialists were right to a certain extent. Erika did begin to speak, but she stuttered. They retained a speech therapist, who came to their home twice a week. There was some improvement, but Renee was still worried.

Another session had ended. Renee was frustrated and started to cry.

"Mommy, please don't cry." Erika tapped her mother's knee and handed her a tissue from the box on the table.

Renee was stunned. The sound of daughter's voice produced more tears.

"Oh, my God! My baby. Father thank you. My precious baby girl is talking."

Erika looked at her mother through her 3-year-old eyes in amazement. *What's wrong with you, Mommy? Just because I'm not talking, doesn't mean I can't.* She took her mother's hand and led her to the piano. She climbed up onto the piano stool, placed her little fingers on the keys and started to play.

"Mommy, look, I can play the piano."

Erika's little fingers glided over the piano keys as she played. Beautiful music filled the air. Erika's head moved up and down keeping time with the music. She was intense and then she smiled. Finally, she stopped playing.

"Mommy, can I have an ice cream cone with sprinkles?"

Renee fixed her daughter an ice cream cone with sprinkles. She also fixed one for herself. In the silence of their smiling eyes, they enjoy their treat. Renee was wiping Erika's mouth, and asked how she learned to play.

"My blood, Mommy." Erika stood up and looked Renee straight in the eye.

Renee was speechless. The piano was a leftover from the previous owner of their penthouse. They decided to keep it and had put it in the alcove off the dining room. Their guests often asked if either of them played. *"Kenny played the trumpet in his high school band; my father and brother are both musicians and Kenny's parents are also talented singers. So, I guess you could say it's in the blood."*

Erika had evidently overheard their conversations.

"Mommy, can I play tomorrow?

"Yes, Erika, you can play whenever you like."

Renee was about to burst. She called Lisa and told her Erika was playing the piano.

> *"Are you serious!? She played that monstrosity you call a piano, and she talked? Praise God! Hold up, how'd she get up there? She's only 3."*

Renee laughed. She hung up and called Kenny.

Kenny was acutely aware of his daughter's impairment and was adamant that Erika attend a private school, most of which required prospective students to be tested before admission. He was the proud papa when Erika's test scores were well above average. She wasn't quite a 'genius', but she was close.

Renee was pleased that her daughter was close to *'genius'* but disagreed with Kenny insofar as her education was concerned. She truly believed Erika would benefit from being around *normal* kids (a/k/a public schools). Kenny was insistent. No child of his was going to a public school with *normal* (a/k/a ghetto) kids and taught by second rate teachers. They compromised --- *sorta*. Erika would attend private elementary and middle schools. There were, however, a few specialized high schools Kenny would consider.

Erika attended the High School of Performing Arts. In her junior year, she began looking at various colleges and fell in love with The Julliard School of Music. She was certain her parents would agree with her choice.

In her senior year, Erika wrote a play entitled *"No Chirping Allowed"*, which was performed before her graduation. The play was about a town that had an abundance of trees of every kind where all types of birds lived. However, some of citizens were annoyed by the chirping birds and cut down all the trees. The town no longer had trees, birds, or shade from the sun. Because of the constant, burning heat from the sun, the town gradually burned itself out.

Most of the audience enjoyed the play, which was followed by a Q&A session. There was a barrage of questions about Erika's motivation/inspiration. Some wanted to know if there was a subliminal message and if so, what was it. Erika was intrigued by the questions and answered them thoughtfully. At age 17, Erika was a young beautiful confident woman. Her stutter was barely perceptible and only occurred when she was extremely nervous. Like her mother, she was slender, cocoa-tan, and had beautiful long reddish-brown hair. Like her father, she was smart, and had a head for numbers.

There were two producers in the house on the night of the performance, who expressed interest in producing her play on Broadway. Erika was ecstatic, as was Renee. Kenny, who managed to make it just before the curtain went up, not so much. Erika told her father that some *really famous* people wanted to produce her play. Kenny congratulated his daughter and spoke with these *really famous* people. At the conclusion of negotiations, the really famous people had lost interest in producing Erika's play. Kenny told Erika the deal wasn't right.

Kenny had high expectations for his daughter. He wanted her to be an attorney, possibly a Supreme Court justice. He also wanted Erika to take over the family business when he stepped down. Of course, he hadn't discussed his plans with Erika, or Renee. As far as he was concerned, he didn't have to.

Unbeknownst to Erika, Kenny had made calls to his alma mater Howard University. Erika had been accepted and would be starting in the fall. Renee and Erika found out about this at the same time. Erika was livid. He knew she had wanted to go to Julliard. He could have flexed his Kenny Wallace muscles with Juilliard as he had with Howard.

Renee didn't approve of her husband's tactics either and she let him know it. Kenny was battling his wife and his daughter. Some days they were both screaming at him at the top of their lungs, on other days they gave him the silent treatment, which for some strange reason was just as unsettling.

Kenny extended an olive branch. He agreed to produce Erika's play, *No Chirping Allowed* at a small theater in SoHo. He swore on an imagery stack of bibles that she would retain full control of all aspects of the production. Erika agreed and the play went into production. From the beginning there were problems. Erika realized she had a lot to learn about theater production. Even with her daddy's money, she was in way over her head and she shut down the production.

Erika began her freshman year at Howard and immediately felt at home. Over Kenny's objections, she took a job with a local theater company. Kenny's admonition *"if your grades suffer..."*, didn't work. Erika's grades didn't suffer. She loved the theater arts department and took full advantage of all it had to offer. Her writing skills were improving and more importantly, she was learning the intricate behind-the-scenes aspects of theater production.

Erika graduated at the top of her class and enrolled in the Howard University School of Law. After earning her law degree, she returned to New York. A short time later, she passed the bar. She was now Erika Wallace, Esq., *and* CEO of K. Wallace Accounting.

CHAPTER 5

Paul Simmons was a tall, slender 30-year-old dark-skinned African-American actor and writer. He had an engaging personality and a killer smile. He had recently been cast on a TV show written and produced by Herman and Tiffany Carter, a successful husband and wife writing team. Herman Carter was a funny-looking man, who walked with a limp and carried a cane. His wife Tiffany was an attractive woman, who was much younger than her husband, but older than Paul.

Tiffany Carter was usually on set and it wasn't long before she came on to Paul. She promised to write more substantial parts for him that the audience would love, thus guaranteeing his longevity as a cast member. Paul always had a way with the ladies. He was also a hustler, and wasn't above prostituting himself for a worthy cause, especially when *he* was the worthy cause.

Tiffany had a ferocious sexual appetite and Paul was more than willing to accommodate her. They usually met at a hotel, however, Tiffany texted Paul to meet her at home. Paul expressed his reservations about meeting at the home she shared with her husband.

"Nothing to worry about." She told him. "My Hermanie's out of town."

Paul called a taxi and went to Tiffany's home. She buzzed him in.

"I'll be right down." She whispered through the intercom. The house was enormous. As Paul was taking it all in, Tiffany greeted him with a deep throat tongue kiss.

"Glad you came." She was wearing a sheer blouse and leggings.

"Me, too." He smiled and winked.

She took him by the hand and gave him a tour of the house, which ended at the master bedroom suite. There was an assortment of fruits and pastries, and bottles of wine cooling in buckets. There was also a large bowl of cocaine and rolled joints on a tray. Tiffany pointed to the goodies.

"Make yourself at home, baby and help yourself. I have to make a call. Be right back." She blew him a kiss.

Paul poured himself a glass of wine, popped a few grapes in his mouth and lit a joint. He stripped down to his boxers and laid across the bed. Tiffany walked back into the master suite naked. She poured herself a glass of wine and took a hit from the bowl of coke. She took another hit, dipped her finger in the bowl and rubbed cocaine on Paul's chest, belly and below. He got aroused and closed his eyes. He felt Tiffany next to him and sucked her cocaine-coated nipples. Tiffany slid onto his body. Then Paul heard a man's voice. A man's voice he recognized. It was Herman's voice.

"Welcome to our home, Paul." The man's voice, Herman's voice said. Herman was naked and was standing in front of the bed holding his custom-made sapphire and tanzanite encrusted cane.

Paul wasn't sure he was about to get a beat down or worse. He pushed Tiffany off him, jumped out of the bed and grabbed his pants. He couldn't find his shirt but headed for the door anyway.

"There's no need to leave, Paul. Tiff and I like threesomes, don't we darling?" Paul was close to the door. Herman moved with surprising agility, and blocked Paul's exit.

"Yes, we do, Hermanie." Tiffany cooed. "Matter of fact, we've been looking forward to this for quite some time." Tiffany was still sitting on the bed with the bowl of coke between her legs. She took another hit.

Tiffany made Paul a proposition: "Come on, Paul, let's have some fun. A threesome and you keep your job."

Paul considered their offer for a moment before he found his shirt and asked Herman to move away from the door. Herman complied and Paul bolted. By the time he got home, he was fired.

The next day, Paul talked to an attorney about commencing a wrongful termination action. The attorney looked over Paul's contract, which basically stated he could be terminated at any time for unspecified reasons; no explanation required. In short, Paul didn't have a legal leg to stand on.

It was a learning experience Paul would never forget.

Paul returned to New York anxious to get reacquainted with the New York theatre community. He put out some feelers which led him to Bruce Hines, a talented Black playwright and director. A few of his plays had received critical (if not financial) acclaim. Bruce had also founded The HineSight Workshop. Writers and actors were clamoring to attend the workshops.

Paul went to a HineSight Workshop. Bruce Hines was intense, yet easygoing. Paul liked him almost immediately, which was unusual for him. He had learned from experience that theater was a dog-eat-dog business. A business in which you don't have friends; rather you formed alliances --- *temporary* alliances with expiration dates.

They were sitting in Bruce's apartment one night having dinner ---- beer and pizza.

"I'm working on something new." Bruce said.

"Writers, write, right?" Paul grinned.

"And, I was thinking we should collaborate. We're always talking about how hard it is for Black actors and writers in this business, as well as our experiences living, breathing and surviving as Black men in America."

Bruce knew firsthand how hard it had been for him to get his first play off the ground. Many producers turned him down without even having read his work. No one was willing to take a chance on him because no one had ever taken a chance on him.

"So, you want to do a play about that?" Paul asked somewhat jokingly.

"Precisely and I think we should write it together. You said so yourself, you're a better writer than an actor. I've read some of your stuff and I agree." Bruce answered.

Paul was flattered. He was silent for about a minute, then he said *Tell me 'Bout it.*

"What?"

"*Tell Me 'Bout it.* That should be the name of the play. We use the expression all the time."

"I like it."

They worked non-stop writing *'Tell Me 'Bout It.'* By the end of the summer, it was finished.

The next step was finding financial backers. Paul suggested they reach out to black-owned businesses. The Kenny Wallace Investment & Accounting Firm was one such business. He sent a solicitation letter to The Kenny Wallace Investments & Accounting Firm, which included a synopsis of the upcoming performance. The letter also offered two complimentary tickets to the donors.

Wallace Investments sent a check for $2500.

"Tell Me 'Bout It" opened off-Broadway. Kenny Wallace used his free tickets and took Erika. Paul knew Kenny would be there.

"I'm Paul Simmons. I wanted to personally thank you for coming and for your support." He extended his hand to Kenny.

"It's good to meet you, Paul. This is my daughter Erika Wallace."

"It's a pleasure to meet you Ms. Wallace."

"Mr. Simmons." Erika nodded.

"Please call me Paul. So, did you enjoy the play?" Paul asked.

"Very much." Kenny answered. "What did you think, Erika?"

"It was okay."

"Just okay?" Kenny was surprised by her response.

"The play has been *'played'* before." She was blunt. "There was nothing new or unique. No new message or focus. Everyone knows how difficult it is for Blacks to be recognized in the theater world, or in the world, period. We need plays that offer solutions, not mere recitations of what we already know. Radical solutions."

"Radical solutions? When did you become so radical?" Kenny was stunned by his daughter's critique.

"I've always been; you just haven't been paying attention."

"Yes, really."

"Beauty is in the eye of the beholder and criticism, good or bad, is always enlightening. Good to meet you both and I hope you'll join us for the after-party." Paul smiled and walked away.

"We're invited to the after-party, Erika. Are you coming?" Kenny already knew the answer.

"No, I'm going to pass on the party. Have fun."

Kenny wasn't prepared for what Erika had just said. What the hell had happened to his daughter? For the first time in a long time, he didn't have an answer. His daughter's opinion was a disappointment, but what the hay. He went to the after-party. He was on his third vodka and tonic and was eyeballing the lead actress Giselle Garcia. Paul was watching Kenny watching Giselle Garcia.

Giselle Garcia was drop-dead gorgeous. She was 21 years old, however, she could easily pass for a high school student. When Kenny first saw Giselle, he took a double take. He was positive he had seen her before. He was racking his brain, and then remembered. She resembled the "15-year-old cheerleader" in the porn films. The video had excited Kenny immensely. He was visualizing Giselle in a cheerleader's outfit. His fantasy was becoming more vivid when he heard.

"Kenny Wallace!" Julia exclaimed.

Coitus interruptus. Dammit! Julia Sherman was tugging at his arm.

"I told Janet it was you. Do you want to know what she said?"

"Julia Sherman. It's nice to see you." Kenny feigned sincerity.

"I told you it was Kenny!" Julia shouts like she's discovered a precious gem. "You owe me 20 bucks."

Julia and Janet Sherman, collectively known as "The Sherman Sisters" are rich hippies, who live in a triplex apartment on New York's Park Avenue and patrons of the arts. They support causes (and plays) that speak to the struggles of the downtrodden. They're rich, philanthropic and extremely boring. Paul was watching and *heard* Kenny's silent SOS.

"Julia, Janet, my two favorite sisters." Paul to the rescue. "And apparently you guys know Kenny." He kissed each of them on the cheek.

"Yes!" they squealed in unison.

"We've known Kenny for over 10 years, right Kenny? Janet asked.

"Wrong, Janet. We've known Kenny for over 20 years." Julia corrected her sister.

"Wrong! Poppa has known Kenny's parents for over 20 years. Me and you..,

"You and I." Julia corrected her sister.

"What?"

"You said 'me and you'. It's you and I, not me and you. That's grammatically correct, right Kenny?"

"Kenny," Julia tugged his sleeve. "settle the bet: when did we meet?

"Well, Julia, I'm not sure." Kenny said.

"Does it really matter *when* you guys met?" Paul interjected. "Think about it?" He used his sincere, convincing voice. "What's more important? What's more significant? The when, or the why?

"Oh, Paul, you are *sooo* right. When you get right down to it, what does it *really* matter?" Julia had tears in her eyes.

"Oh, Paul, your insight; the profundity of the question speaks volumes." The other Sherman sister said. There were tears in her eyes, and she was agreeing with her sister for the first time in years.

"No matter the when, the where or the why, ladies, it's always good to see you both." Kenny said. He kissed each one on the cheek. The Sherman Sisters giggled in unison and hurried over to Jan Hughes, another patron of the arts.

Between the incessant chatter of the Sherman Sisters in his ear and the fantasy bubble in his head of Giselle Garcia in a cheerleader uniform bursting, Kenny's felt like he was in a twilight zone. Or, maybe, he just had too much to drink. Whatever it was, Kenny knew he needed to get the hell out of there and headed for the door. Paul caught up to Kenny as he was leaving.

"Hey, man, thanks for coming. Appreciate the support. It appears we have a lot in common."

"What makes you say that?" Kenny asked. His voice was tight. He had snapped out of it. The Kenny Wallace Investments & Accounting Firm switch had been turned on.

Paul instantly detected the *switch* and switched gears. He glanced in Giselle's direction and nodded. Just like that, Giselle was walking toward them. Paul introduced his lead actress to Kenny.

"It's a pleasure to meet you." Giselle smiled.

"The pleasure is all mine." He smiled and hoped the thoughts running through his head weren't projected onto his face.

It was the beginning of the alliance between Kenny Wallace and Paul Simmons, albeit for different reasons.

Paul needed financial backers for future productions. Kenny could be an excellent resource. Kenny needed women who looked like teenage girls. Paul could be an excellent resource.

Kenny gave Paul his business card. "Call me, I have a few ideas that might interest you."

"Tell Me 'Bout It" continued its run for nearly a year. Kenny attended many of the performances after which he and Giselle would spend time together. He also invited her to join him on some of his out-of-town trips. It was a comfortable arrangement. Kenny was super-generous, which made watching porn flicks and reenacting whatever role fulfilled his fantasy of the night more tolerable for Giselle.

Paul and Giselle were having dinner after a performance.

"Kenny wasn't in the house tonight. Everything okay?"

"Yea, things are okay." She was not surprised by the question. She knew Paul was aware of their relationship. "He's at a business seminar."

"That explains why I didn't see him tonight."

"Yeah, which means I don't have to watch porn tonight."

"Porn? You and Kenny watch porn?"

"Yep. He's addicted to the stuff. He can't get it up or off unless I wear a cheerleader's outfit."

"Get out! A cheerleader's uniform?" Paul dropped his fork. "Kenny? I figured him for a strictly missionary-position man."

"Well, you figured wrong."

"No shit. I guess it's true, you can never judge a book by its cover."

CHAPTER 6

"Tell Me 'Bout It" had its last performance in Washington, D.C. at one of Howard University's campus theaters.

In addition to being CEO of K. Wallace Accounting, Erika was also on the advisory board of the theatre arts department at Howard U and spent a great deal of time commuting between Washington, D.C. and New York.

When her father called and said he was coming down for the play's final performance, she was surprised.

"Really. You saw it in New York. You liked it that much?"

"Yes, I did. Plus, it'll give me an opportunity to spend some time with my favorite daughter."

"Your favorite daughter? Don't you mean your *only* daughter? Unless, you're trying to tell me I have a sister."

"Stop being so dramatic. You're my one and *only* daughter."

"Mommy coming, too?"

"No, baby. She's busy working on some new products with Lisa."

"I'm driving down tonight, and I'm at the Hyatt. Care to have lunch with your ole man tomorrow?"

"Yeah, sure, Daddy. Text me in the morning. Love you."

"Love you too, baby. Holla at ya later."

"Really, Daddy? You're gonna *'holla'* at me? Bye." Erika smiled. Gotta love him.

Kenny checked into the Hyatt and called Giselle.

"Hola, Popi, Como estas?"

"I've missed you." Kenny answered.

"You at the Hyatt?" She asked.

"Yes, I am. How soon can you get here?" He poured a drink from the minibar in the room and slipped off his loafers.

"Sorry, Popi, not tonight. Paul called a rehearsal. He wasn't happy with the last performance. Says we were dropping lines, missing cues, sloppy. Says he's been way too lenient, and we need to be whipped into shape."

"Really? The performance in New Jersey?

"No. The one before Jersey in Pennsylvania?"

"I didn't notice."

"That's because you only see me." Giselle laughed.

"That's true for the most part, but I do pay attention. I'm not saying I catch everything, but I do have a discerning eye."

"Oooh, a *'discerning eye'*. I like that Popi. My baby's got mad skills."

"And *my* baby's got *muy* skills too."

"When's your birthday, Kenny?"

"What?"

"When's your birthday?

"February. Why?"

"I'm buying you Spanish for Dummies. You're brutalizing my language. Shame, shame, Popi."

"Si, si, *muy* apologies."

"You're hopeless."

"I may not speak Spanish, but I do speak the language of love."

"Since when are we in love, Popi?"

"Since the first day I saw you. Didn't you see the look on my face?"

"I saw you looking at my ass and my tits. That's what I saw."

"Exactly, the look of love, my dear. I'll see you tomorrow then?"

"Not sure about that either."

"Why?" His voice was tight.

"Look, I don't know all the particulars, but Bruce and Paul are splitting up. Bruce has been talking to some backers in LA who want to produce his stuff."

"That's great, but what's that got to do with you?"

"I'm going with Bruce."

"When?"

"After the performance tomorrow night. I'm not sure if I'll be at the party.

"You screwing Bruce?"

Silence. Giselle was annoyed. This was supposed to be an adult, no-questions-asked relationship. Now this married-ass clown had the nerve to ask me who I'm screwing.

"Silence speaks volumes. I'll take that as a yes."

"Bye, Popi." Giselle hung up.

Kenny swallowed his drink and fixed another one. He was trying to decide how he felt about what Giselle just said. It wasn't like he expected it to last forever, right? Easy come, easy go.

The alarm in his attaché case went off reminding him to check the security cameras he had installed in his home. Initially, the cameras were installed in the elevator and around the entranceway and terrace. Later, he had another camera installed in the master bedroom. Renee did not know about the camera in their bedroom. As a result, she was unaware the bedroom camera captured her and Lisa in all their glory, as they were that night.

"I knew it!" Kenny exclaimed.

He had long suspected there was more to their *friendship.* His suspicions were finally confirmed. He would download the footage later. Something in his gut told him it could be useful.

Kenny went to the hotel's Olympic-size pool and swam 3 laps. As he came for air, a man in a suit approached the side of the pool.

"Good evening, Mr. Wallace."

"Good evening." Kenny removed his goggles.

The man bent down and the gun inside his jacket pocket was visible.

"Lance Barrington sends his regards and asked me to personally remind you of your indebtedness. Consider this a courtesy call, Mr. Wallace. Enjoy your swim."

Kenny lingered in the water for a few seconds. He was more mad than scared. How dare that son-of-bitch send me a *personal* reminder.

Lance Barrington and Kenny Wallace attended the same middle school. At first glance, it appeared they couldn't be more different and would have little in common. Kenny was an only child of two professional parents, living on Long Island. Lance Barrington and his brother Gerard grew up in the Bronx and were raised by their single mother who worked in a laundry/dry cleaning plant. What they did have in common were their academic achievements. Kenny and Lance both excelled academically. Gerard, Lance's brother, was a star athlete.

Kenny and Lance's paths crossed when Kenny started running his three-card-Monte scam in middle school and

Lance was selling drugs. Because their *businesses* were not in conflict, there was no animosity and they got along. *Laissez-faire* capitalism at work. Kenny *retired* his scam when he got to high school, but Lance's drug enterprise grew.

Kenny had smoked weed in high school and did coke in college, under the guise he needed it for all-night cramming sessions. He and Renee often smoked together and he and Giselle often sniffed coke together, under the guise the coke would enhance his sexual performance. He was lying to himself. The fact that it had the exact opposite effect, escaped him.

Lance Barrington was still a drug dealer, but his customers were no longer his middle school classmates. Rather, they were rich people of every ethnicity who liked to get high.

Lance was also a shrewd businessman. The fact that he was a drug dealer was irrelevant. *All* business is business, after all, particularly if its profitable, and Lance's businesses were. However, Lance was acutely aware of the limited shelf life of his *profession* and wanted to live to see his grandchildren. He knew there was longevity (and profitability) in diversification.

Lance owned two properties: a brownstone in Harlem where he lived and an old warehouse in Riverdale. The Riverdale warehouse became The Barrington, a restaurant frequented by his upscale coke-sniffing and gambling clients. Thanks to his connections (and the fact that he had never been arrested), he was able to get a liquor license. The Barrington was an elegant two-story restaurant with a gourmet chef in the kitchen. The main dining room was on the ground floor with two well-stocked bars on each side of the room. Lance's office was in the back of restaurant on the ground floor, which made access to the parking lot easy. The two rooms on the second floor were for the high-stakes poker games.

Everything was legit, except of course the gambling.

Lance was careful about who he invited to his club. He sent invitations to his business owner friends whom he thought would be interested in having a place to discretely enjoy a friendly game of poker, a good meal, have a drink, etc.

Lance had read about the Kenny Wallace Investments & Accounting Firm and gave his former classmate a call. To his surprise, Kenny answered the phone.

"Of course, I remember you, Lance. How have you been"?

"I'm well. Word on the street is that you're a magician."

"Really? Last I heard, I'm a miracle worker." Kenny laughed.

"Yeah, that too." Lance agreed. "I own The Barrington."

"The Barrington?"

"It's a restaurant in Riverdale. Why don't you stop by? We can have a few drinks, dinner if you like and catch up. I'd also like to talk to you about investing.

"Sure. I'll stop by Friday evening. Love the name, by the way; sounds classy. Text me the info."

Kenny had heard about The Barrington. One of his clients told him about a new restaurant where patrons could enjoy a friendly game of poker after dinner. However, his client never mentioned who owned the restaurant and he hadn't connected the name to Lance Barrington, the drug dealer from middle school.

Kenny went to The Barrington and was impressed. It wasn't long before he was hooked on the high-stakes poker games, and he usually went home a winner. However, he did have a proverbial bad night or two. He had also set up a modest investment portfolio for Lance.

Kenny began experiencing a streak of bad luck and was losing big time. Lance noticed Kenny's losses. Nonetheless, he advanced Kenny $50,000. Despite the advance, Kenny was still losing money. Lance had given Kenny a week to make good on the loan. Kenny was faced with a serious financial crisis which needed to be rectified immediately. He reviewed some of the investors' accounts to determine which ones could be manipulated without detection. He transferred $50,000 from the Renee's Hair Care portfolio and wired Lance the money.

He left a voice message for Erika to let her know he was at the Hyatt and was looking forward to seeing her. He checked the market before falling asleep.

The next afternoon, Kenny and Erika met for lunch. Kenny greeted his daughter with a kiss on the cheek. She looked good and she looked happy. Kenny was wondering if there was someone special in her life, preferably a young man. He was praying sexual deviance was not hereditary.

"Hey, Daddy. I am *soooo* glad to see you." Erika was energized. She kissed her father on both cheeks. "And before you ask, I've followed up on the new accounts and everything's up to date."

"I know."

"You checking up on me, Daddy?"

"No. Well, may just a little. You're doing a lot."

"I like being busy."

"Well, you certainly seem to be in a good mood."

"Yes, I am. I'm having lunch with my Daddy at the FireDome. How very VIP, Daddy."

The waiter took them to their table and gave them menus.

"I've always liked their veggie burgers. What are you having?"

"Steak and eggs and a FireDome Bloody Mary.

"Daddy!"

"What?"

"Steak and eggs? Oh no. Not on my watch." Erika waved her finger.

"Not on your watch? What does that mean?"

"It means you're not going to have a heart attack while I'm watching. Mommy would kill me."

"Okay, okay. Can't have your mother kill her daughter because her father ate meat." Kenny laughed at his humor.

"No, we certainly can't have that." Erika frowned. "I think you should have a veggie burger, too."

"Okay, I'll have a veggie burger with a side of curly fries,"

"Sweet potato fries."

"Okay, sweet potato fries and a FireDome Bloody Mary."

"There you go! And I'll have a FireDome Bloody Mary too."

A compromise on lunch having been reached, they ate and talked.

"So, what's up? You still the advisor of the theater department?"

"Yes, Daddy, I am." This was a sore spot for Kenny. He was afraid she might resign as CEO for K. Wallace Accounting.

She knew her father well. "Don't worry, I am not resigning from K. Wallace. However, there is something I need to share."

"Do I need another drink?" He asked.

"I'm in love, Daddy."

"So, what's his name? Where's he from? What does he do?" Kenny bombarded her.

"It's not he, Daddy."

Kenny was holding his breath. Please, God, please. It can't be in the hereditary, can it?

"Does your mother know?" He croaked and took a large gulp.

"You alright?"

"Yes."

"Of course, Mommy knows. Matter of fact, she told me to go for it. And thank God she did. You know the saying: 'Mommy knows best?'"

"I thought it was *father* knows...,"

"How dare you! How chauvinistic! Your mother, your grandmother, me and Mommy trained you better."

"Calm down, Erika. I was trying to be funny. Apparently, I failed. I'm sorry. So, fill me in. Who are you in love with?"

"A magnificent, but old, rundown theater. I going to buy it. Don't worry, I have some money of my own, so it won't cost *you* too much." She grinned.

"Good. I'm glad to hear that." Kenny wiped the beads of sweat off his forehead.

"Are you sure you're okay? Oh wait." Erika laughed. "You thought I meant was in love, and knowing you, with a man."

"Well, yeah, but I guess buying an old rundown theater is good too." He was clearly relieved.

"Yes, it is Daddy. Bon appetite!"

CHAPTER 7

Erika and Kenny went to the last performance of *Tell Me 'Bout It*. Erika noticed Paul had made substantial changes --- *for the better*. Maybe her father shared her critique of the play with Paul. The audience enjoyed it too. The cast and director got standing ovations. Because this was the final performance, there was a party afterwards. This time, Erika went with her father. She noticed how chummy Kenny and Paul were and how the cast knew him as well. She made a mental note to check whether her father had any financial interest in Paul's theater company beyond his initial donation.

"Daddy, what's going on?"

"Why do I feel like I'm about to be interrogated?"

"Because you are. Answer the question. What's going on? Everyone seems to know you."

"I'm a people person, Erika. People like me."

Paul's rescue radar was on and he was at Kenny's side before the conversation continued. He had two glasses in his hands.

"Erika, what a pleasure to see you."

"It's nice to see you too."

Paul handed her one of the glasses in his hand.

"Thanks." Erika sipped. "Cavullo Savignon Blanc?"

"Yes."

"Ticket sales must be up."

"Yes, they are." Paul nodded.

He is one good-looking man. Erika wondered why she hadn't noticed that before.

"So, what did you think of the play this time? Kenny told me you panned it the last time." He was thinking about how pretty she is and wondered why he hadn't noticed before.

"You obviously made some improvements, and it shows." Erika said.

"That's high praise coming from you."

"Why is that?"

"Because you're a Howard U. theater arts grad. Actually, I'd very much like to talk to you about some new stuff I've working on when you have time." He was staring at her intently. And then he smiled.

Erika felt her cheeks heating up, turning beet red. OMG, I'm blushing. Please God make him stop. And, please God, don't let me stutter (which she tended to do when she was nervous and/or excited).

"Well, I am pretty busy, but..."

"I see you two are talking shop." Kenny interrupted. They had both forgotten he was still standing there.

"Sorry, Kenny, my bad." Paul said. "I would like to get Erika's opinion on some new things I'm working on. However, she hasn't said yes yet. Perhaps, you can put in a good word for me." Paul smiled.

There's that damn smile again Erika was thinking.

"I can vouch for him, honey; and that's my cue." Kenny looked at his glass. "Time for a refill. Erika, make sure you try the Cavullo Savignon Blanc, and tell me what you think. Cavullo Selections is a subsidiary of the Morgano Group."

"I know. Actually, that's what I'm drinking. It's pretty good."

"Glad you agree." Kenny said and went to the bar.

"I understand you're thinking about relocating to D.C." Paul resumed the conversation.

"How did you know that? Erika asked.

"Your father told me."

"My father told you. Do you two talk on a regular basis?" She was slightly annoyed.

"It's nothing sinister, counselor. Mostly business, however, occasionally your name does come up. He's really proud of you, as well he should be. You've accomplished a lot in a relatively short period of time. And mean it when I say *you.*"

"Explain."

"Okay, counselor: you haven't relied on your father to get ahead. You stand on your own two feet. It's an admirable quality. A lot of rich kids think they're entitled and don't have to work for anything." There was a slight edge to his voice, which he noticed and instantly corrected.

"This is a great space. A great institution. But you already know that. Four years undergrad, then Howard Law." Paul said, hoping he's succeeded in changing the subject.

"What school did you go to?"

"Street University."

"Okay, I'll bite: what's Street University?"

"I know it's lame. I went to City College. I used to say Street U because I thought I was being deep. Thought it was cool, but now, well, it's just lame."

"Yes, it is." Erika laughed and relaxed. "Where did you grow up?"

"New York for the most part. But I've also lived in LA."

"Native New Yorker. What part?"

"Okay, here's the pedigree: I was born in Harlem Hospital. That's in Harlem."

"I know where Harlem Hospital is."

59

"Just checking. Both my parents worked for the Post Office and we lived in Uptown Terraces, which is a private housing development in Harlem. I went to Taft High School and graduated from City College." Paul was standing at attention looking her straight in the eye. Then he smiled. "TMI?"

"You haven't said anything about a wife and children or siblings."

"I'm an only child and I'm not married."

"Children?"

"Ah, counselor. I was wondering if that would get pass you. Guess not."

"Well?"

"I have no children."

"At least that you know of, right?"

"Oh, I'd know. Trust me on that. So, what do you say? Will you take a look at my new stuff?" His eyes were piercing.

"Sure. Give me a call next week. We can set something up then."

"Splendid." Paul smiled. He heard his name being called. "Excuse me, I'm being summoned. My apologies."

"No apologies necessary. After all, you've accomplished a lot, and I do mean *you*." Erika smiled and walked away before Paul does.

Erika looked around for her father. She spotted him and the young woman who was the lead in the play. From where she was standing, it looked like they were arguing.

"I'm sorry, Kenny. No, you know what? I'm not sorry." Giselle said.

"Then why are you here? I thought you were leaving right after the show."

"Paul asked me and Bruce to hang out for a while. We're leaving after the party." Giselle started to walk away. Kenny grabbed her arm.

"You owe me, Giselle."

"Let go of me and I don't owe you a damn thing. You got what you paid for."

"Daddy, is everything okay?" Erika was behind him.

Kenny turned abruptly. "Yes, dear. Everything's fine. Giselle, this is my daughter, Erika."

"Nice to meet you." Giselle said and walked away.

Erika glared at her father and walked away.

From the look on Erika's face, Kenny knew she had overheard his exchange with Giselle. He thought she was going to call Renee, but he didn't try to stop her.

Although the thought crossed her mind, Erika didn't call Renee. However, knew she had just witnessed *a lovers'* spat. She also knew her parents' marriage had been on the rocks for years. But that was grown folk business, as Grandma Wallace used to say. She checked her watch. She could still make the reception hosted by the law department. Professor Jamal Williams had texted her earlier and invited her. She had texted back a 'maybe.' She went to the bathroom to check her makeup and heard voices coming from the stalls.

"Can you believe that old married-ass clown had the nerve to tell me I owed him."

"Girl, you have got to be kidding. He should be glad you went along with him and all his kinky shit."

"Then he had the nerve to introduce me to his daughter.'"

"Are you serious?"

Erika left the bathroom before she heard the response. Paul was standing there.

"Are you alright? It was almost as if he knew what she had just heard.

She nodded.

"I'm glad I caught you. I wanted to give you, my card."

"Thanks." She took his card and headed toward the elevator.

He was about to say more, when Giselle and her friend came out of the bathroom laughing. "Hey, Paul, great party. I didn't get a chance to talk to you, but I'm glad you're okay with me and Bruce." Giselle said.

"Yeah, yeah. I'm okay with it." He said as he watched Erika get on the elevator.

CHAPTER 8

Kenny returned to New York the day after the play closed. Erika returned later in the week and worked from home on the K. Wallace Accounting accounts. She had her own apartment within her parents' penthouse and used two of the rooms as her home office. Thus, she was able to avoid Kenny until the monthly meeting that required all the execs to be present. Erika had suggested a virtual meeting, but Kenny said no. For the most part, the meeting ran smoothly, although there was some back-and-forth difference of opinions between Kenny and Erika, the virtual meeting concept being one of them. Kenny didn't like the idea of virtual meetings. *I like being able to reach out and touch the troops. Look my people in the eye.*

Albert Miller, the oldest accountant in the world, agreed with Kenny, which was predictable. Albert Miller always agreed with Kenny. Erika often wondered if Albert ever had an original thought in his life.

As expected, the Morgano Group account was on the agenda. Kenny advised the board that the account needed to be restructured. More importantly, the personnel/payroll records needed to be updated. He also advised the board that Jeremy's hiring practices had also come under scrutiny.

Erika asked why that was their responsibility. "We handle their books. We're not their HR department."

"Look, the Group is growing, and The Cavullo Wine Selections' account needs to be updated." Kenny answered.

"I get that. Cavullo Wine in pulling in more revenue, but that has nothing to do with Jeremy and I told you before, he's a loose cannon. He treats the staff like shit in general and disrespects the female staff in particular. It's just a matter of time before someone slaps a discrimination or harassment lawsuit on his ass."

"Well, in that event, he can retain your services, counselor." Kenny responded.

There's an audible hush in the room. Kenny realized he had gone too far. "I'm joking, Erika."

"Is there anything else you'd like to *joke* about? How about the one about the old man and the aspiring actress?" Erika asked.

It was obvious to everyone that the tension between them was more personal than business-related.

"Well, I think..." Albert Miller coughed before he finished his sentence. "Excuse me." He said in his raspy voice. He popped a cough drop in his mouth trying to clear his throat and started to choke. Kenny jumped up and patted Albert hard on his back. Albert fell forward. In a swift move worthy of baseball outfielder, Larry Mathews caught Albert, preventing him from hitting his head on the table. Albert coughed up the cough drop along with his upper dentures. The cough drop, and his dentures landed on the conference table.

"A revised version of the Heimlich maneuver. "Erika said. "Thanks, Larry. Make sure Albert gives you a reward for saving his life." She was trying hard not to laugh.

Meeting adjourned.

Erika went to her office. She logged onto her computer and opened the Morgano accounts. She saw her father walking toward her office. His cellphone rang. He turned around when he heard the ambulance sirens. Erika wondered if someone called an ambulance for Albert.

Erika turned off her computer and left the building. She started walking, not exactly sure of where she was headed.

"Erika." Paul Simmons caught up to her. "I thought that was you. How's everything? I was just on my way to a meeting with your father."

"Paul, how are you?" She remembered there was some new business on the agenda that Kenny wanted to discuss. Putting two and two together, she figured Paul must have been the new business.

"I thought I might be meeting with you too."

"We had a medical emergency and the meeting ended earlier than expected."

"Oh, sorry to hear that. Nothing too serious, I hope?"

"No, fortunately it wasn't too serious." Erika suppressed the urge to laugh again.

"Glad about that, however, I was looking forward to meeting with you guys. Is there any way you could still make that happen?" Paul smiled.

There's that damn smile again!

In theory, she could. She knew her father was still at the office, as were the other board members. She had a feeling whatever Kenny wanted to discuss regarding new business was already a done deal. Presenting Paul to the board was merely a formality.

"I'll text him and let him know we're on our way to his office." Erika texted her father.

The meeting was short. Paul had formed his own production company and Kenny had agreed to act as his financial advisor. As she suspected, the deal was done. Paul offered to take them to lunch.

"Thanks, Paul, but I have another meeting. However, I'm sure Erika would be happy to have lunch with K. Wallace's newest client." Kenny and Paul shook hands and Kenny excused himself.

"I hope he didn't put you on the spot. If you would prefer not to have lunch, I understand." Paul smiled.

"It's okay."

"Great. Where would you like to go?"

They walked to a restaurant not far from the office. The regular lunch time crowd was gone, so the place wasn't crowded.

"What would you suggest?" Paul asked as he perused the menu.

"The burgers are good. Although I don't eat red meat too often. But every once and in while it can't hurt, I suppose. The grilled chicken salad is also good. So is the grilled salmon with Hollandaise, or just lemon. I usually get one or the other. I get the veggie burger, when I have a taste for meat. It's pretty good too." Erika realized she was rambling and abruptly shut up.

Paul laughed. "That was quite thorough. Have you ever worked here?"

"No." I, I, I, eat here often." She was stuttering and her cheeks were red.

"Think I'll go with the grilled salmon. I'm cutting down on red meat too. He smiled, reached across the table and put his hands over hers. "What will you have?"

There's that damn smile. "The grilled salmon." She stood. "I'll be right back." Erika fled to the restroom. Snap out of it, girl. You can handle this she tells herself. And she does. She returned to the table and was all business.

"I'm sure you can appreciate that I haven't had a chance to

review your financials. I'll need a few days to look them over. I assume you gave my father the necessary documents, i.e., certificate of incorporation, tax ID, etc."

Paul stared at her. The 360-degree change in her demeanor was disconcerting to say the least.

"I understand. I took the liberty of ordering lunch. Hope you're not offended.

"Why would I be offended?" She realized her tone. "I'm sorry, it's been a helluva morning."

"Well in that case, would you like a glass of wine, or something stronger, perhaps? He gave her his bad-boy wink.

"Yes. White Zinfandel."

"Excellent choice. It pairs well salmon." He summoned the waiter and ordered two glasses.

"You're a wine connoisseur?" Erika asked.

"A wine drinker." Paul answered.

"Me, too." Erika giggled.

Over lunch, Paul told Erika about his plans for his production company. "I want to produce and direct my work, as well as the works of others. A lot of good writers and actors need an inexpensive venue where their work can be performed."

"I'm with you on that. In fact, I'm in negotiations to purchase an old theater in Washington, D.C."

"Hey, that's great. Are you looking for an apartment in D.C., as well?"

"I'm still trying to decide. My mother thinks it's a good idea."

"I understand your mother owns a very successful beauty supply company." Paul saw the inquisitive look on Erika's face. "Yes, before you ask, your father told me."

"He tells you a lot.

"We talk. Mostly about investments. He's a smart man, but you already know that.

"Renee's Hair Care. That's my mother's company. It started as a hair care product company and now sells all kinds of beauty supplies and products for men and women. She and Lisa are doing quite well."

"Lisa?"

"Lisa Taylor and my mother are partners. Way back when, Lisa hired my mother to sell her beauty supplies. It's a long story."

"Rags to riches?"

"Yeah, sorta."

"Those are the best kind. You should write a play about it."

"Maybe I will."

"It could be our first, or maybe second, play performed at your new theater."

"*Our*?"

"Yes, Erika. *Our.* I can help you write it." He said confidently.

Erika laughed. "You can *help* me?"

"Yes, Ms. Howard U-Fine-Arts-Grad, Esq. I'm gonna help you. Mark my words, Ms. Howard U-Fine-Arts-Grad, Esq., I'm gonna help you do a lot of things."

"I admire your confidence."

"I know." He smiled.

"I was being sarcastic, Paul."

"I know. Thing is, Erika, we're a match made in heaven. We're both on the same artistic, creative expression track." He smiled again. "And I love sarcasm."

"Well, this has been interesting. Thanks for lunch." Erika said. "I'll call you in a few days."

"It been a pleasure." Paul helped Erika out of her chair.

They left the restaurant and were standing on the sidewalk. It was a bit awkward. Paul wasn't sure if he should shake her hand, kiss her on the cheek or hug her. Erika was just as perplexed. What to do, what to do?

"Where you headed; home or office?" Paul asked.

"Home."

"Can I help you catch a cab?"

"Sure."

He hailed a cab.

"By the way, did my father offer his financial expertise to any of your cast members?"

"I don't know. Maybe."

She got in the cab and waved from the window.

Erika was intrigued by Paul. She was even more interested in learning the extent of his *friendship* with her father. She knew Kenny supported African American-owned companies, but she felt there was more than that with Paul Simmons.

The incident she witnessed in Washington had made her super suspicious. What she overheard in the bathroom was disturbing. She didn't see the faces of the women who were talking, but she was sure one of them was the woman her father introduced her to and the lead actress in the play. That would also explain why Kenny had seen the play as many times as he had and why he and Paul were friends.

Paul caught the subway uptown to his apartment in Harlem. He was living in the same development where he had grown up, which had since been converted into condos. His parents bought their apartment and the one next door to it at insiders' price. They had retired and moved south. Paul had possession of both apartments.

Paul was intrigued by Erika as well. She was smart and pretty in a way different from the women he normally thought to be pretty. He was attracted to her. She was also Kenny Wallace's daughter and that could be problematic. Her query about Kenny offering financial advice to any of the cast members made him wonder if she knew about Giselle Garcia and her father.

Paul had always been interested in cultivating a relationship with Kenny Wallace. After all, the man was rich and famous. He just wasn't sure how this could be accomplished. When he noticed Kenny's attraction to Giselle at the reception party, he saw an opening. Over time, Paul became aware of Kenny's marital infidelities, as well as Kenny's *kinkiness*. In fact, he had been a facilitator of sorts. From time to time, Kenny asked Paul if he could use his apartment for private meetings. Paul knew Kenny was lying, but he gave his keys anyway. Ordinarily, that would not have concerned him. If a man was cheating on wife, that was between the man and his wife. Perhaps they needed a marriage counselor. Paul was a hustler, not a marriage counselor. And it was because of Kenny's financial support that *Tell Me 'Bout It* ran as long as it did. One hand was washing the other.

Nonetheless, Paul was feeling conflicted. Mother of God, was he growing a conscience? Or worse, was this woman who, when she stuttered looked so cute getting next to him*??*

CHAPTER 9

It had been a week since her lunch with Paul Simmons and Erika was sitting at her desk when her cell phone rang.

"Yes, of course, I understand. Thanks."

The call from the realtor she had been so anxiously waiting for delivered bad news: the DC theater had been sold to developers. She was aware that the developers were interested in the property, but she was certain she had a good shot.

She was staring at her cellphone when it rang again. It was Paul Simmons. She started not to answer but changed her mind.

"Erika Wallace."

"Hey, babe, it's me." Paul said.

Despite her deflated mood, she laughed. "Babe? I thought we were partners."

"We are partners, babe and I have something I'd like to show you."

"Really?"

"Yes, really. It's a building in Harlem."

"A building in Harlem?" She repeated.

"Hear me out, babe."

"If you call me babe one more time, I'm gonna hang up."

"Okay, okay. I won't call you babe. There's a building in Harlem I think would make a great theater. Better than the one in D.C. We should check it out."

"Okay."

"Wow, that was easy. No ten thousand questions?" He was surprised.

"Do you want to show me the building or not, Paul?"

"Let me get the keys from the super. I'll call you back."

"Text me the address, I'll meet you there at 4."

Paul was standing on 132nd Street in front of a three-story mixed-use brick building with an attic and a basement, which has been vacant for several years. The surrounding neighborhood consisted of housing developments (the condo where Paul lives being one of them); a supermarket, a few mom-and-pop grocery stores, a nail salon, and a laundromat. There was a church on the corner and two fast-food eateries. It was good location from a business perspective: lots of pedestrian foot traffic, street parking, a nearby subway stop and a bus stop in front of the building.

They entered the building through the ground level and Paul outlined his plans. Erika liked the space and was impressed with Paul's overall plans. Paul had the realtor's business card in his hand.

"I'll set up a meeting if you're interested in the property."

Erika took the card and put it in her pocket. "I'll call in the morning. I need to think it over."

"Fair enough. There's something else I'd like to show you."

Erika laughed. "You show me yours, and I'll show you mine?"

"Why, Ms. Wallace, you have a dirty mind."

Erika was still laughing. "You have no idea, Mr. Simmons."

"Intriguing. I don't live far from here and one of my favorite Chinese restaurants is around the corner. We can order take-out and I have a pretty decent wine collection. I figured we could have a bite while you read my latest piece."

"Sounds good."

Paul was amazed she was being so amenable.

Erika was equally amazed. Paul had no way of knowing that the D.C. theatre deal had fallen through, yet here he was telling her about a theater in Harlem. *When God closes a window, he opens a door.*

Paul and Erika dined on Chinese food and wine. Paul put on some music and Erika got comfortable. She kicked off her shoes, sat cross-leg on the sofa and started reading Paul's play *'After'*.

Paul watched her as she read his play.

She pushed her glasses to the top of her head and strands of hair cascaded down her face as she sipped wine and smiled intermittently turning the pages. Paul took this as a good sign. At one point, she put the script down and laughed out loud. Paul had to know:

"Where are you?" he asked.

"Page 12."

Paul flipped through his script to page 12. "Oh yeah, that's some funny shit. Glad you got it."

Erika finished the script.

"It's good Paul. You should be proud."

They had spent hours discussing his play, his plans and drinking wine.

"Whoa, look at the time. I should be getting home." Erika said. She unfolded her legs, lifted herself up from the couch and stretched. She was a bit off balance and Paul jumped up to catch her. He put his arms around her and kissed her.

Erika spent the night at Paul's. They made love and the next morning, they had breakfast in bed. That was their beginning.

Erika caught a cab home. She felt like a schoolgirl who had been kissed for the very first time. Erika's boyfriend track record was short. Her last foray into the love zone was uneventful. In fact, most of her love forays had been uneventful.

But this felt different.

Later that day, Erika called the realtor. The asking price wasn't too bad. It seemed like a good investment. There weren't many theaters in the area despite the abundance of talent in the community.

Erika was mulling over the idea when Renee stepped off the elevator of their penthouse apartment.

"Hi, dear. Everything okay? Renee kissed her daughter's cheek.

"Everything's fine and I have news. Sit down."

"Good or bad news? Do I need a martini first?"

"Better yet, how about a glass of red?" Erika suggested. "Cavullo Wines has a new line, and I brought a few bottles."

"Sounds good."

Erika poured two glasses and told her mother the deal in Washington, DC had fallen through.

"Oh baby, I'm so sorry. I know you had your heart set on the theater."

"When one door closes, God opens another. And this is where the good news comes in."

"Okay. I'm listening and you're right, this is good. Looks like Cavullo Wines have a winner with this one."

"Yes, it is good. The Savignon Blanc is also a winner." Erika agreed.

Erika told her mother about the building in Harlem she was thinking about buying and briefly mentioned Paul Simmons.

Renee noticed Erika was surprisingly upbeat, despite

having lost the theater in D.C. She assumed this Paul Simmons probably had something to do with it.

"So, you won't be getting an apartment in D.C.?" Renee asked.

"I don't need to now."

"What about the theater department at Howard? I thought you wanted an apartment to cut down on commuting back and forth." Renee said.

"You sound disappointed." Erika said.

"I'm concerned. That's what mothers are for."

"And daughters are inquisitive." Erika countered.

"Especially my daughter." Renee laughed.

"That's right. Now, is there something else going on?" Erika remembered the conversation she overheard in the bathroom.

"Okay." Renee sighed. She knew this conversation was long overdue, but it was still hard. "The truth is your father, and I are having problems. Our marriage is falling apart. Correction, our marriage has fallen apart."

"Have you considered counseling? Erika asked.

"It's too late for counseling. We're way past that. The passion died a long time ago."

"Are you sure there's nothing you can do?"

"Your father has been cheating on me for years, Erika."

"How did you find out? Did he confess? Did you hire a private detective?"

"How I found out isn't important." Renee was momentarily taken aback by Erika's questions. It was as if she already knew about her father's infidelity.

"Are you divorcing?" Erika asked.

"No, not at the moment. It's complicated, but I'm sure it's an eventuality."

"This is a lot to take in."

"I know it is, and I'm sorry. However, what's more important is that you have an opportunity to fulfill another dream. Your father and I have fulfilled ours."

"Oh God, Mom, you sound like you're about to die."

"Not yet. But I don't know what the future holds for your father."

"Oh my God. This is going from bad to worse. What else aren't you telling me?"

"There's nothing else to tell. And as far as I know, your father is in good health. Now, switching gears, do you have enough money to buy the Harlem property?"

"I do, but it would drain my bank account, which is something I'd prefer not to do."

"Does your father know about this?"

"Yea, I told him about it when we were in Washington."

"When were you two in Washington?"

"Homecoming weekend. Actually, there was a lot going on that weekend. You and Lisa had your launch party, and the play closed the same weekend."

"What play?"

"Paul's play. Daddy was one of the backers." Erika said. "As a matter of fact, Paul is interested in us being partners." Erika slipped in that last tidbit.

"What kind of partners? Does he have any money? You can't be too careful, Erika. There's a lot of evil people in this world."

"I hear you." She wondered just how much she really does

knew about Paul and her father. "I'm surprised daddy never mentioned him."

"Your father has lots of friends he's never mentioned. Paul is probably a nice guy, but I don't think you should mix business with pleasure."

"Who said anything about pleasure?" Erika's cheeks were turning red.

"Your cheeks did. I know you, Erika." Renee laughed. "I'll help you purchase the property, with no strings attached."

"I don't know what to say."

"Say thank you. Okay, now that's settle, tell me more about this Paul."

"Well, like I said, he's a playwright. He's also an actor and director. I met him at the opening of the play Daddy backed."

"How was it?"

"The first time I saw it, I didn't like it. However, when I saw it again in D.C., it was a lot better. It was obvious Paul had made substantial changes over the course of the run. And I just read another piece he wrote, entitled *After*. It's really good."

"Do you know how many times your father has seen the play?" Renee was making mental notes. She wanted to divorce Kenny, however, the terms of her pre-nup were not in her favor. She needed leverage to strengthen her bargaining position.

"The play ran in a few cities and Daddy saw most of them."

"So, where's Paul from and how old is he?"

"He's from New York, but he's lived and worked in LA."

"And, how old is he?"

Erika heard the question, but the truth was she didn't know how old he was. She had never asked.

"If I had to guess, I'd say 30 maybe, a little older." She was trying hard to keep her voice flat and her face relaxed.

Renee raised an eyebrow. "In other words, you don't know. Did you even ask? Is this pretty-boy playwright, actor, writer and director that good?"

"Ma!" The façade was gone. She was tempted to say, *hell yea, he's that good*. "What kind of question is that?" She asked indignantly.

"Don't Ma me. I know when something's going on with you, Erika. And if he's friends with your father, I'd be super skeptical." Renee was blunt. Perhaps too blunt and she realized she needed to be careful. She wasn't ready to tell her daughter she's been sleeping with Lisa for years.

Erika was feeling uncomfortable too. She wasn't sure if she should tell her mother what she knows about her father. *Grandma Wallace's wise words: stay outta of grown folks' business.* The only difference, of course, was that her mother already knew her husband was cheating on her. What she overheard in the bathroom was now confirmed. But Erika heard her mother say they weren't getting a divorce --- at least *'not at the moment.'* Putting on her attorney's hat, she was sure there something more sinister afoot. Was her mother having an affair, as well? Don't ask, Erika, don't ask. *Grandma Wallace's wise words: stay outta of grown folks' business.*

"I like Paul. He's smart and he's a good writer. And, yes, he's a pretty-boy. I know he and Daddy have been friends for a while now and that Daddy set up an investment account for him. He did alright financially with the play, but I'm sure the money is practicably gone. He does own a condo and sublets his parents' condo. Bottom line, he needs another profitable project."

"Or a rich girlfriend." Renee said derisively.

"You didn't raise a dumb child, as you are so fond of saying." Erika poured them another glass. "I'll be careful though."

"That's all I ask. Now, when do I get a look at my new investment and future son-in-law.

"Ma!"

"Switching gears, how's it going at K. Wallace Accounting?"

"It's going. Most of the clients are happy with us and have recommended us to others." Erika answered.

"What about the Morgano Group?"

The Morgano Group had been a K. Wallace Accounting client for years, and Erika handled the day-to-day management of the account. The Morgano Group was primarily a wine and liquor distributor. It also owned Jeremy's Pub, a restaurant that mostly hired college students who needed jobs to help with tuition. As such, frequent changes in personnel were not unusual. However, Erika was suspicious of some of the expenditures and believed the Group's business practices were one step away from being illegal. She told her father what she suspected, but he refused to drop them as clients.

It took some time, but The Morgano Group did come under investigation. Thanks to Beverly Andre.

CHAPTER 10

Beverly Andre – 2011

Beverly Andre was a cute, petite 19-year-old young woman with dark brown hair which she wore in a short pixie-cut. She had received a small scholarship to Vantage College however, she still needed a part-time job to help with expenses.

"Beverly Andre." The director of Student Employment Services at Vantage College was calling her name.

"Beverly Andre?" the director called again. "Going once..."

"Yes, yes, I'm here." Beverly gathered her things and moved through a row of chairs toward the director's desk.

"Have a seat, Ms. Andre."

"Thank you."

The director was looking at a computer screen. "Okay, let's see what we've got here. How are you adjusting? I see you're in the Agnes Dorm."

"Yes, I am, and everything's just fine." That was the first lie of the day.

"Is that so? Students usually complain about Agnes Dorm."

"Well, I, I guess it...,"

"Save your breath, Ms. Andre. Being politically correct is an admirable quality, *sometimes*. Now, have you done any wait service?"

"Wait service?"

"Have you ever been a waitress or worked at McDonald's?"

"I've worked for Uncle John's Barbeque Pit." Second lie of the day, *sorta*. Her father and his brother John (her uncle) cooked and sold barbeque dinners on the weekends in the summer in the park across the street from their house. They would set up a "pit" (which was actually a ten-gallon black metal barrel) and cook the best barbeque ribs in the Bronx. When the lines of customers got too long (as they often did), her father made her help taking orders.

"Uncle John is your uncle?"

"Yes, ma'am." *True.*

"I remember Uncle John's Barbeque Pit. It was back in the late 80s, right? Is he still cooking?"

"Yes, he's still cooking, but in Florida. He moved there after he retired." Beverly was like: you have got to be kidding me! What are the odds that out of all the college counselors in all the colleges in the world, she would be talking to one who knew her uncle?!

"Ah, too bad. That was some good barbeque. You don't suppose he'd send his niece a care package?" The counselor laughed.

"I don't see why not. I'm still his favorite niece." Not a total lie. All Uncle John's nieces *and* nephews are his favorite.

"Okay, then let's see about finding you a job. Jeremy's Pub is always looking for people. The owner Jeremy Morgano is good about hiring our students. I'll send him a text and let him know you'll be coming in for an interview. What's a good day and time for you?"

"Right now."

"I'll tell him to expect you tomorrow afternoon around 3. That work for you?"

"Yes, tomorrow afternoon around 3 is good for me."

Beverly wanted to make a good impression and showed up for her interview at Jeremy's Pub an hour earlier. Jeremy Morgano interviewed Beverly. She wasn't his type, but he needed a waitress and hired her. He told her the salary wasn't much, but she could make up the shortfall with tips.

On her first day on the job, Sandy Hawkins introduced herself. Beverly remembered seeing Sandy Hawkins on campus.

Jeremy asked Sandy to help Beverly get started. '*Show the kid the ropes.*' Sandy went over the menu with Beverly and how to take orders. She told her to pay attention to customers' bill, as that's how her tips would be paid. Sandy told her she could make a lot of money, if she knew how to play the game.

Beverly was assigned a section of tables where she waited on customers who were not considered regulars. Vernon Rivers was the exception. He always sat in her section and was one of Beverly's regulars. He was also a good tipper and often complimented Beverly on her appearance. Beverly was polite. She thought Vernon was a typical middle-aged man going through a mid-life crisis.

Beverly reported for work one afternoon and Vernon was sitting in Sandy's section. Beverly was pissed. Sandy knew Vern was *hers*. Beverly noticed that Vern had been drinking a little more than usual and Sandy was being more flirty than usual. When Beverly asked Sandy why she had pilfered Vern, Sandy told said her wallet needed a boost. She wasn't exactly sure what Sandy meant, but decided not to ask any more questions.

Two days later, Bev clocked in and Vern Rivers was sitting in a booth in her section. He ordered lunch and a drink. When

Bev brought his drink to the table, he grabbed her hand and pushed it down to his crotch.

"If you want a tip, massage my balls."

"What?!" Reflexively, Beverly withdrew her hand and the drink spilled in his lap.

"Lick it up." Vern laughed.

Before she had time to react, Jeremy was at the table. "Hey, Vern, sorry about that. I'll get you another drink on the house. Wait for me in the kitchen, Bev."

She was shaken. Would the spilled drink come out her check, or worse, would the spilled drink cost her her job?

Jeremy met Bev in the kitchen; he was blunt:

"Vern wants to do you. Be nice to him and you can keep your job. Matter of fact, you can make a lot more money." Jeremy patted her cheek.

She wasn't naïve and knew exactly what has just happened. She took off her uniform and threw it in the garbage. She was angry and charged out of the kitchen and ran directly into Erika Wallace.

"Whoa, girl, where's the fire."

"Sorry, I didn't see you."

"Obviously." Ericka responded. "An excuse me could do nicely."

"Excuse me." Beverly said as the tears began to flow.

Erika reached into her bag and handed her a tissue. "Here."

"Thanks."

"I'm guessing Jeremy made his move?"

"What?"

"Did he threaten to fire you if you didn't play nice?"

"I'm sorry, have we met?" Beverly wiped her face.

"Indirectly. I'm Ericka Wallace of K. Wallace Accounting. We handle the restaurants' financial records. Jeremy is clever enough to keep the books clean, but his overall business practices are in the toilet. In short, he's pimping out some of the waitresses."

"Isn't that against the law? Beverly asked.

"Yes, it is, but nobody's calling the cops." Erika sarcastically answered her.

"I need this job. I'm in college."

"As are most of the waitresses working here, which is why they're such easy targets and Jeremy knows it."

"I'll find another job. There's plenty of restaurants around here."

"FYI, Jeremy and/or his family own most of them."

"I can't." Beverly said almost to herself shaking her head.

"What's your major?" Erika asked.

"Journalism, with a minor in business management."

"Interesting. Look, if you can write..." Ericka started to say.

"I'm told I'm good. I was the editor of my high school paper and I've written a few pieces for local newspapers." Beverly interjected.

"I admire your confidence." Ericka laughed, rummaged through her bag and handed her a business card. "It's a public relations firm. They're looking for an intern, and they're legit. Good luck."

Beverly shoved the card into her backpack. She never went back to the restaurant, but she did find employment:

She baby sat for a college professor's children. The kids were obnoxious and dangerous. Plus, there was Cindy, the family cat. The kids had heard that cats had 9 lives and were on a mission to disprove the myth. She discovered she was allergic to cats when she tried to rescue Cindy from death by hanging. She saved Cindy, took an allergy pill, and tendered her resignation.

Her next job was in security. The security world, she learned, was now high tech and she loved it! Gone were the days of old men with a ring of keys jangling from loose fitting trousers, dozing off at a reception desk console, barely able to stand let alone "walk" the premises.

Reception areas were now custom-made security stations equipped with state-of-the-art computers and surveillance cameras. Jangling keys had been replaced with key fobs. The money was good and the hours flexible. She liked the job.

She also discovered there was a connection between security and investigative journalism. Nothing was private, secret, or sacred.

Beverly graduated from Vantage College with a degree in journalism. Her first job was at a local TV news station as an entry level assistant copy writer.

As expected, she was doing a little bit of everything. One day, a few hours before airtime, the weather girl threatened to quit if she didn't get a raise. She figured her request would certainly be granted, inasmuch as the weather forecast slot aired fairly early in the broadcast and they wouldn't be able to find a replacement so quickly. The weather girl figured wrong and was fired. Without missing a broadcast beat, Beverly was the new weather girl. The fact that she had no meteorological credentials didn't matter. She looked good on camera and could read the teleprompter.

Despite her misgivings about being just another pretty, perky face, she liked being the weather girl. It gave her exposure, limited as it was, and enhanced her credentials, limited as they were. Nonetheless, she knew she had to move on. She wanted to be an investigative reporter. She was out to make a name for herself—a household, universal name.

Beverly bounced from one station to the next, from one city to the next. She didn't mind relocating. The fact that she had no love life was a trade-off she was willing to accept. A few brief "romantic" interludes along the way and she was good to go.

She came close to a "serious" interlude with Dave Jackson, a cameraman who worked at the same station. He was smart, handsome, and compassionate; the kind of man Beverly eventfully hoped to marry. The operative word of course was eventfully. Bev was worried, however. She realized that Dave Jackson was becoming a chink in her armor. She and Dave were without a doubt falling in love with each other. She was in agony, dueling with her emotions. Then fate stepped in.

Beverly reported to work one morning and was told the station was under new management. By the end of the day, everyone had been fired. However, in a gesture of goodwill, the station gave the newly fired a list of stations that were hiring.

Her next job was with a small newspaper. It wasn't TV, but she was an optimist, believing that everything happens for a reason. The editor and Elliot Osbourne, owner of *Do Tell* magazine were friends. Beverly met Elliot Osbourne when he stopped by the paper. Elliot had been more than a little impressed with Beverly. She was cute and according to his friend, had potential. Elliot's *I-bet-she-does* look caused his friend to tell him that wasn't what he meant, but he told Elliot he was welcomed to take his best shot. For reasons Elliot couldn't quite put his finger on, he decided not to. However,

Beverly stayed in Elliot's memory bank. The paper folded the following year, and she was once again looking for a job. The editor suggested that she contact Elliot Osbourne. Beverly thanked him but doubted that Elliot would even remember her let alone hire her.

She was wrong.

She called Elliot and he agreed to see her. By the look on his face as she entered his office, she knew that he did remember her, and she knew she had the job. For Elliot, it was love at second sight and he hired her on the spot. Sadly, he realized early on that their friendship would be strictly platonic. His friend had been right: Beverly was a good writer and had potential. Elliot taught Beverly a lot and they became good friends.

Elliot Osbourne believed that everyone had a story to tell, and everyone wanted their story to be told. Beverly was sitting in Elliot's office one evening and told him about what she had experienced working as a waitress at Jeremy's Pub when she was in college. As she was telling the story, she realized how angry she still was. So did Elliot. He suggested she do an expose. She was excited. This was the type of reporting she always wanted to do. Plus, it might expose Jeremy Morgano and his illegal enterprise.

She knew at the outset that most of the people she worked with had graduated and would be difficult to locate. Nonetheless, she put on her investigator's cap and was able to locate Sandy Hawkins. After the *how have you been chit-chat,* Beverly got to the point: she was writing an article about the exploitation of college students who needed to work in order to pay their tuition. She was focusing on restaurants in general and Jeremy's Pub in particular.

"Good luck with that." Sandy said and ended the conversation. Sandy had recently finished med school and didn't want to get involved.

Sandy Hawkins had always admired Beverly for not going along to get along. In fact, she wished she had done the same thing, but this wasn't the time for regrets; but a little revenge might suffice. After some soul-searching, she contacted Beverly. She agreed to talk providing Beverly wouldn't publish her name or image. Bev agreed and they met for lunch. Sandy told Beverly what she knew:

Jeremy's side hustle happened by accident. He had rented out the back room to a local college basketball team for an end-of-the-season party. Nothing too extravagant; just beer and burgers. Jeremy also agreed to provide the hostesses. The coach and one of Jeremy's hostesses decided to have a private party in Jeremy's office. Jeremy walked in on them. He wasn't sure what he should do, however, before he had a chance to thoroughly process the situation, the coach thanked the hostess, stuffed a hundred-dollar bill in her bra, and placed two one-hundred-dollar bills in Jeremy's hand. The coach told Jeremy he was sitting on a gold mine. He had a lot of friends who would pay for this stuff. Jeremy Morgano had found a new source of revenue.

Beverly asked Sandy how she knew all this. Vernon Rivers was the coach. Beverly asked whether Sandy thought Vernon would talk to her. Sandy didn't think that possible as Vernon had died of a heart attack a few years ago.

Sandy had confirmed that Jeremy was using the restaurant to recruit girls (and guys) for his other enterprise, but she didn't think anyone from the college was in cahoots with him.

"I had a scholarship, but it didn't cover my living expenses." Sandy explained.

"Yeah. How well do I know."

"I heard Jeremy's Pub was hiring waitresses and applied for a job. I handed Jeremey my resume which he threw on his desk without a glance. Instead, he told me to try on the waitress uniform. If it fit, I had the job."

"Really, that wasn't my experience." Bev was perplexed. She was sure she would not have forgotten something like that.

"No offense, but you're not the right body type. I mean you're cute enough...,"

"Gee, thanks."

"Don't take it the wrong way. Just not enough T&A."

"Tits and ass?"

"Cute *and* smart."

"Gee, thanks."

"Well, I knew Vern Rivers wanted to do you."

"How'd you know that?"

He told me. Matter of fact, he wanted a threesome."

"A what?"

"Come on girl, you have to know what a threesome is."

"Of course, I know what it is." Beverly nodded. "He was getting a little *too* familiar. I remember seeing him sitting in your section. To be honest, I was mad with you. Then he was back in my section and you were gone. Word was you had been promoted.

"I was working the private parties. I don't have to spell it out for you, do I?"

"No, you don't."

"Good. Anyway, I was working a private party and one of the

'customers' wanted a service I wasn't willing to perform. I mean he was into some real freaky shit. The customer complained, and Jeremy literally kicked my ass to the curb."

"Oh, my God. He got physical?"

"I'm going to assume that's rhetorical. I was bruised and battered, but luckily, no broken bones. *And,* the son-of-a-bitch refused to pay me."

"That's terrible; worse than terrible. I thought you had dropped out of school."

"I transferred to a college back home and graduated. I went on to med school and I'm now an intern at Mercy General."

"Did you tell your parents what had happened?" Beverly asked.

"Both my parents had died by that time."

"Sorry. No other family?"

"I had to tell my brother. Jeremy had beaten me pretty badly. My brother came and got me. He wanted to call the police, but he backed off after I told him the full story. Although I had a helluva time stopping him from going after Jeremy."

"My God, Sandy, I'm so sorry. I had no idea."

"Well, God is good. He protected my sorry, know-it-all butt. Look, I've got to run. It was nice seeing you and good luck with your article. And remember, I'm an anonymous source; no names, no pixs, deal?" She extended her hand for Beverly to shake, changed her mind and hugged Beverly instead. "Thanks for lunch."

Beverly stayed at the restaurant for a few minutes collecting her thoughts.

What Sandy left out was that Jeremy raped her and shortly thereafter, she found out she was pregnant.

Beverly went back to the office and told Elliot what she had learned.

"Like I said, you need to write your story, tell your truth. Don't worry, kid, I got your back."

Beverly raised questions about legalities: Could the magazine be sued? Could Elliot be sued?

Elliot was silent for a minute. He got up from his chair and walked across his office, hit a button on the wall, which opened to his bar. He took a bottle of Reserve Jack Daniels from the shelf and two glasses. "Don't ever doubt me. Beverly. If I say I got your back, I got your back." He filled one glass.

"Sorry, Elliot. I didn't mean to imply...,"

Elliot raised his hand. Stop. He walked to the window, swirled his glass, admiring how the Reserve Jack glistened in the sunlight streaming in from the window.

"I know you know, I drink Jack. What you don't know is that I have my Reserve Jack. *'Reserve Jack,'* by definition is special and forgive the redundancy, reserved. I drink it on rare occasions and share it on even rarer occasions. This is one of those rare occasions. I'm gonna share my Reserve Jack with you, providing you write the story." Elliot poured her a glass of Reserve Jack.

Bev nodded. The clinking of glasses solidified the deal.

Beverly wrote the (her) piece on prostitution and college students. Keeping her promise to Sandy, she was careful not to name names, but skillfully left identifiable clues. The story went viral and it did catch the attention of the authorities, which led to an investigation of the restaurant and Jeremy Morgano. Not surprisingly, Jeremy Morgano knew people who knew people in high places, and the "investigation" ended before it began, but not before the paper received death threats and Elliot's car tires were slashed. For Elliot, this was little more than an annoyance, rather than a real threat, and his insurance replaced the slashed tires. Beverly, however, was alarmed and shaken. Elliot told Bev she should be flattered. *'Death threats are good --- it means you're being heard. Put on your big girl panties, Bev; this comes with the territory.'*

Beverly worked for *Do Tell* magazine for another two years, and as of 2016, Jeremy's Pub was still in business.

CHAPTER 11

Erika Wallace usually handled the Jeremy Pub account electronically. However, she did make random in-person visits, which infuriated Jeremy Morgano.

When she arrived that afternoon, she was told Jeremy wasn't available. Undeterred, she barged into his office and found Jeremy seated at his desk with his eyes closed. The sudden intrusion caused him to jump up. His pants were down, and he was fully exposed. A young woman was under the desk. Jeremy's sudden movement caused her to bite down.

Jeremy screamed. "Ow! You, dumb bitch. Get out."

The young woman fled from his office.

Jeremy tried to zip up, and his 'meat' got caught in the teeth of the zipper. He screamed again.

"I told you about just showing up."

Erika left. She was furious and wanted to do something about Jeremy. But what?

On the drive back to her office, Beverly Andre popped into her head. She remembered reading and being impressed by Beverly's article in Do Tell magazine. More importantly, it confirmed what she already suspected was going on at Jeremy's Pub.

Erika knew Beverly was now a talk show host on The Rick Cherokee Show. She called Beverly and reminded her that they had met when Beverly was a waitress at the Jeremy's. She also offered belated kudos to her on the article on the Pub and related her latest encounter with Jeremy. Beverly agreed that the man was a pig.

"Maybe you could do a show. A follow up to your article. I've watched some of your interviews, you're good."

"Thanks." Beverly said. "I have an idea. How would you like to be a guest on the show?

"You sure you want me and not my father?" Erika responded. Usually, it was her father who was newsworthy.

"I mean you. You're perfect and you've accomplished so much. However, a daughter and father interview would be sensational. There aren't many stories like you and your dad's. We could talk about the difficulties women confront in the workplace and on campus. It could lead into a conversation about the Jeremy saga."

"Let me think about it, okay? I really don't know how much I can say or should say about Jeremy and the Morgano Group. They're clients. I'll have to run this by our legal department."

"You're an attorney." Beverly said.

"Yeah, but they're clients. Let me check. Better safe than sorry. I certainly don't want to be disbarred.

"Alright. At least you're not saying no. Actually, it sounds like a 'yes' to me. Talk to your Dad and tell him I said hello."

"You know my father?" Erika was surprised.

"I met him in Philly. A friend of mine was in a play called *Tell Me 'Bout It*. It was a good play. I figured your Dad was one of the producers, but my friend said no. She said he and the director were good friends."

"I'll get back to you, Bev."

CHAPTER 12

RICK CHEROKEE

Rick Cherokee is a 6 feet 5 inches tall, good-looking, ex-professional basketball player, with smooth cocoa brown skin and hazel eyes. Three years ago, Rick had been invited to speak at a charity event sponsored by businessmen who needed tax write-offs and politicians who liked to have their pictures taken with super star athletics. Nobody was fooling anybody; sponsors got their write-offs and the proceeds (at least some) went to the charities.

Rick made his speech, shook hands, and smiled for the cameras. He excused himself and walked to the lobby of the hotel. He took a selfie with the valet who brought Rick's rented BMW to the hotel entrance and then headed to the airport. He never made it.

His BMW was hit head-on.

Rick was airlifted to the nearest trauma center. He was in a coma, fighting for his life. Both his legs were shattered; his right arm and four ribs were broken.

The driver of the car that hit Rick was Allen Metcalf, son of a prominent businessman. Allen Metcalf sustained a concussion and a broken wrist. Responding police officers found an open bottle of vodka on the front seat and a significant amount of cocaine in the glove compartment of the Metcalf vehicle.

Treating physicians told the Cherokee family Rick would

survive, however his playing days were over. In fact, it was a miracle that he wasn't paralyzed.

Treating physicians told the Metcalfs their son's chances for a full recovery were good. The police commissioner told the Metcalfs there was also a good chance their son could go to prison. Kathy Metcalf told her husband through clinched teeth her son was not going to jail because of some nigga: *'You better fix this. 'I don't give a shit if he's a basketball player, or not. The drugs were probably his anyway. He should have been the one they arrested.'*

Louis Metcalf did not need his $1500-an-hour attorney to tell him his son was in serious legal trouble. With his three priors, Allen could do time.

In addition, the press was all over this. Allen Metcalf's arrest record was on Facebook and the court of public opinion had already convicted him. Many questioned why he was allowed operate a motor vehicle in light of his three DUIs. Sport fans, both black and white, were calling for the death penalty. Community leaders and clergy were demanding justice.

Rick commenced a personal injury lawsuit. Almost a year to the day of the accident, Rick settled his personal injury lawsuit for $10.5 million.

The criminal case against Allen Metcalf was still pending. After using various delay tactics, a firm date for the trial had been scheduled. In an ironic twist of fate, Allen Metcalf was killed by a drunk driver who slammed into the car transporting him to the courthouse.

Justice prevailed and Rick won his civil case. Divine intervention resolved the criminal case.

Rick underwent several surgeries. Because he was in

excellent shape, his body healed relatively quickly. However, mentally he struggled and there were many dark days. Hoping to boost his spirits, he and parents flew to the Bahamas for a 7-day vacation at a luxury resort.

Rick wasn't sure if it was the warmth of the sun and Caribbean waters, or the pretty young women who offered their services (including food and wine), but he had a good time. His *I-can-do-anything* spirit had been restored. When he got back home, he started on a vigorous rehab regimen.

Before the accident, Rick had had his eyes on a piece of property in upstate New York. He called his real estate agent and told him to make it happen. In matter of months, Rick Cherokee was the owner of a large estate in Westchester county.

Rick was offered coaching positions, but that wasn't his thing. Apparently, he was still relevant, because he was regularly booked as a guest on talk shows. He realized how much he liked talking on talk shows. That's when the idea for the Rick Cherokee Show hit him.

Despite his celebrity, none of the networks were interested.

Rick was undeterred. He started Cherokee Media and installed a state-of-the-art multi-media studio on his Westchester estate.

Rick read lots of newspapers and magazines principally because his name often appeared in them. He had subscribed to *Do Tell* for years and remembered reading the piece on college students and prostitution written by Beverly Andre. She was young and attractive and would appeal to the audience he wanted to reach.

Rick contacted Beverly. He told her about his concept for the Rick Cherokee Show. The show would focus on trends and issues that affected viewers under 40. He was straight, no chaser. He wanted a host (preferably a young female) who not only looked good on camera, but who wouldn't be afraid to go for the jugular, if necessary. He wanted to do probing, thought-provoking shows and needed a host who would ask provocative questions.

He asked her if she would be interested in being a host.

She assured Rick she could do the job and thanked him for the opportunity to show him. They set up a meeting.

Beverly told Elliot Osbourne she had been approached by the Cherokee Media. Elliot was familiar with the Cherokee Media. More specifically, he was familiar with Rick Cherokee, the ex-basketball player and of course the accident that ended his career. He wasn't sure if the show had longevity, but he wished her the best.

Prior to the interview, she researched her prospective employer. She knew Rick Cherokee had been a basketball player and vaguely remembered reading about his accident.

She found the professional photos of Rick. Um, Beverly thought, not bad, not bad at all. She also watched video clips of his TV appearances. He was affable and didn't come off as cocky. Still, she wasn't sure what to expect. Conventional wisdom dictated he would be arrogant and full of himself. The Rick Cherokee on camera could be a completely different Rick Cherokee off-camera.

In keeping with her custom and practice, Beverly arrived at the Cherokee Media's Westchester offices earlier than her scheduled interview. An assistant told her Rick would see her shortly. Beverly waited 30 minutes before she was finally ushered into his office. Rick greeted her warmly. Despite her initial annoyance, she liked him. They talked and Rick gave her a tour of the studio after which she signed an employment contract with Cherokee Media Group.

Rick put Beverly on the air almost immediately. He had a hands-off management style, however when he was displeased, she knew it. Conversely, when he was pleased, she knew that as well.

One morning, she walked into Rick's office. Sitting on the sofa was Macklin Hawk (nee Macklin Hawkins), a/k/a Mack, The Hawk. Beverly apologized for the intrusion and turned to leave.

"No, please come in, Bev." Rick said. "I want you to meet Macklin Hawkins. Mack, this is Beverly Andre. She's the host of ...

"I know who she is." Macklin Hawk got up from the sofa and extended his hand, "Hello, Ms. Andre, it's a pleasure to meet you."

"Hello, Mr. Hawk." That sounded so stupid, '*Mr. Hawk*'.

"Bev," Rick said, "Mack and I have lots to discuss. I'll talk with you later, that okay?"

"Sure, it's nothing that can't wait. Nice meeting you." Bev said to Macklin as she was leaving.

"Pretty woman." Macklin sat down on the sofa.

"Yes, she is." Rick agreed.

Mack the Hawk, was America's latest heartthrob. He was a good-looking, muscular, light-skin Black man, whose brown hair, under certain lighting, shimmered with red highlights. Macklin, like many *overnight sensations* began his acting career doing off-off Broadway theater. He was now the star of an action-packed TV cop show.

Macklin was also an avid basketball fan and went to see Rick play whenever his team was in town.

Rick was a fan of Macklin's show and wanted him to be a guest on his show. Rick had his people call Macklin's people. This was their first meeting.

"I usually have my agent handle this kind of stuff, but I wanted to talk to you one on one." Macklin said. "To be frank, I'm not big on 5-minute fluff piece talk shows, but your shows are good, and I enjoyed watching you play."

Rick smiled. "Thank you, and I'm not big on fluff either. I'm also quite selective about who I ask to be guests. I'm not trying to sound arrogant, but not everyone gets on my show and believe me when I say I have a long list of wanna-be guests."

"I hear that. I'm sure your team does background, but if I agree to do your show, there are restrictions. Macklin said.

"Of course."

"My agent, as well as the show's producers, will send over the do's, and don'ts.

"SOP."

"Right; standard operating procedure." Macklin nodded in agreement.

"So, can I assume we have deal?" Rick asked.

"Pretty much."

"I'm glad. You're a fan favorite, but I must warn you, my audience is very discerning. They dislike fluff *and* bullshit." Rick led him to the door.

"I do have one request." Macklin stopped.

"Name it."

"I want Ms. Andre to do the interview." Macklin said.

"No problem."

Rick chuckled to himself. This should be fun. If Macklin thinks Bev will let his pretty-boy superstar persona get in the way of her doing a thorough interview, he had better think again.

CHAPTER 13

Beverly had watched Macklin Hawk's TV show and was surprised that the writing was as good as it was. The cast was diverse and not portrayed in the usual stereotypical TV-cop series fashion. Certain aspects of the show were predictable, but overall, the show offered its audience intriguing plot lines. Hawk's character was a sexy wheelchair-bound police officer. Rumor was that one of the producer's son had been injured in the line of duty (the specific duty was never specified) and was in a wheelchair; hence, the inspiration for the show. Hawk's character was a composite of the producer's son and *Ironside*, the first famous TV wheelchair detective. Another rumor was that Hawk's character would regain the use of his legs. The show's social media followers were split 50/50 on that story line.

Beverly read the background info compiled by the Cherokee staffers, as well as the material supplied by Hawk's people. The Cherokee research, however contained an interesting tidbit that was not part of the show's background info. Macklin has a sister who is a physician—Dr. Sandra Hawkins. Beverly Goggled Dr. Sandra Hawkins. Dr. Hawkins was her old college friend Sandy Hawkins.

Bev called Sandy.

"You have reached the office of Dr. Sandra Hawkins. I'm unable to take your call at the present time. At the sound of the tone, please leave your name and number and your call will be returned as soon as possible. If this is a medical emergency, please hang up and dial 911 immediately." BEEP.

"Dr. Hawkins, this is Beverly Andre. Please call me at 347.555.2111."

Sandy's last patient for the day had canceled and she had gone to the gym. She finished her routine and checked her messages. She heard Beverly's message, and was annoyed. Now what?

It had been over a year since she had provided Bev with information for her exposé on Jeremy's Pub. Bev had kept her word and not mentioned Sandy. Nonetheless, Jeremy had sent her a message: he would kill her if she talked to the authorities. Sandy told Macklin. It didn't really matter, however, because she was never contacted by the police or the media.

She knew she wouldn't be able to reach Macklin until later. She would call Beverly after she had spoken to her brother.

Sandy and Mack had always been close. Even though she was older, Mack acted as if he was her older brother. They grew up in a small rural town. Sandy was hard to miss. She was a high-yellow-Black woman with curly red hair and was 5 feet 10 inches tall. While many thought Sandy would be America's Next Top Model, she doubted it. She loved her curves and had no intention of starving herself just to fit into a size zero dress. Sandy, in a word, was voluptuous.

This caused her brother to be extremely protective.

Their parents, Lester and Inez Hawkins, had worked at the lumber mill since graduating high school. Her mother Inez had also taken night classes at a community college and earned an associate's degree in accounting. When the bookkeeper at the mill retired, Inez applied for the job. She was given the usual run-a-around. Inez was beginning to make noise about racial and gender-based discrimination. *'I can work the line, but not in the office. Nothing's change: House nigga/field nigga.'*

Around the same time, many of the workers were getting sick; some were dying. Suspicions grew that something in the mill was killing them. They were right; the killer was asbestos. Lawsuits were commenced against the mill for asbestos-related illnesses and/or deaths.

The last thing the mill needed was more legal scrutiny. Fearing a discrimination action, Inez Hawkins was hired as the bookkeeper.

Inez came home one evening from work and found Lester on the bathroom floor hugging the toilet vomiting. Inez screamed and tried to lift him to his feet. After what seemed like an eternity, she managed to get him to the bed. Lester was sweating profusely and started to vomit again. When the vomiting finally stopped, Lester fell back onto the bed exhausted. He told Inez to call an ambulance. Lester Hawkins was diagnosed with mesothelioma and died two weeks later.

The family was devastated. Lester's life insurance policy paid for funeral expenses and Inez was able to pay off the mortgage. Inez started having headaches and her blood pressure was high. Her doctor reminded her she had been under considerable stress and was grieving the loss of her husband. Under the circumstances her symptoms weren't unusual. Six months later, Inez suffered a stroke and died.

Sandy and Macklin were both in college. Days before her passing, Inez made her children promise they would stay in school. They sold the house and returned to their colleges. Macklin got a job stocking goods at a home supply store. Sandy got a waitress job at Jeremy's Pub.

CHAPTER 14

Beverly confirmed that Macklin Hawkins a/k/a Mack the Hawk and Dr. Sandra Hawkins were brother and sister, however, she wasn't sure what to do with this new information. The fact that Dr. Sandra Hawkins and Macklin Hawkins had not been *outed* as brother and sister suggested neither of them wanted it to be made public.

Beverly was not into *gotcha* journalism. She respected a persons' right to privacy, particularly when exposing someone wasn't germane to the story. And even sometimes when it was, she didn't. It was important that her sources trusted her, and Sandy had been a source.

Mack's guest appearance had not been locked down and experience had taught her that things in this business could change on a whim.

She and Rick had talked about the Hawk's interview. She could tell that Rick was clearly looking forward to it. For the time being, Beverly decided not to divulge what she had learned about Macklin Hawkins and Sandy. She normally didn't withhold information from Rick, but for some reason, she felt justified in doing so this time.

What she did share was her idea about Erika Wallace and her father Kenny Wallace, Jr. being guests on the show.

"How do you know them?" Rick asked.

"I met Erika when I was working at Jeremy's Pub. Her father's accounting firm handled the Morgano books, which as you may recall owns the pub. I literally ran into Erika the same night that sleaze-ball Jeremy tried to recruit me."

109

"Interesting. You never mentioned anything about the Wallaces and the Morganos being connected." Rick said.

"I never thought about it like that. The Morganos are clients."

"How well do you know the father?"

"I don't *know* him. I *met* him at a play in Philly a friend of mine was in."

"And you didn't know Kenny Wallace was Erika Wallace's father?

"I didn't know when I first met her. Like I said, it was the same night Jeremy tried to recruit me. I was angry and literally ran into Erika in the kitchen. She saw how upset I was. In fact, she said she was wondering how long it would take for Jeremy to make a move. She asked me about my major and gave me the business card of a PR firm that was hiring."

"So, she got you a job?"

"No. I never called the PR firm. And I had not spoken to her until she called me the other day."

"And...??"

"She told me about a recent encounter she had with Jeremy."

"Don't tell me he tried to *recruit* her?" He asked.

"Wish he had; we'd be talking about his demise." Beverly laughed.

So, what's the interview going to be about? Erika Wallace, heir to the throne of one of the most successful Black-owned companies? Or Erika Wallace, attorney, activist and defender of women's rights? Or, at home with Erika Wallace?" Rick asked.

"Why not all of the above. She's a multitasker. I mean think about it, that's who she is. And, I might add, she's not the only multitasker." Beverly was getting warmed up.

"Like you."

"Yea, like me and thousands of others like me."

"With a rich daddy?" Rick asked.

She wasn't sure if he was trying to be funny. You never could tell with him.

"Of course, not. But she's not relying on her rich daddy. True, her father's money is an advantage."

"*You think?*" Rick's sarcasm was obvious.

"What do *you* think? Is it worth pursuing?"

"Yeah, maybe."

"I'm surprised you don't know Kenny Wallace." Beverly said.

"I know who he is."

"Everyone knows who he is. That's not what I meant."

"I know what you meant, Beverly."

Beverly was silent for the moment. She wasn't quite sure what was going on, but the vibe had definitely changed. "Alright, then. I guess we'll talk later." She left his office.

Rick had met Kenny Wallace when he was in his rookie year. He had been invited to a party at an upscale hotel hosted by one of the team owners. Kenny Wallace was there along with the usual partygoers: wealthy fans, team investors, a few politicians, groupies and 'working girls'.

Rick had heard that Kenny Wallace was the Black Financial Wizard. Rick already had an investment advisor, but he believed in supporting Black-owned businesses. He had intended to call Kenny, but here he was in the flesh, standing at the bar with his arms around two young women. Rick had also heard that Kenny Wallace had a reputation of liking young girls and from the looks of things, he was living up to his rep. Rick introduced himself to Kenny and said he wanted to talk to him about investing. Kenny excused himself to the ladies and took Rick

111

aside. He told Rick he had just made arrangements to hook up with the two young girls and said he would call Rick later, unless of course he wanted to join the party. Rick declined the offer and Kenny never called him.

Beverly's cellphone rang. It was Sandy Hawkins, M.D.

"Hey, Sandy." Beverly said.

"What's this about, Bev? I helped you before and the investigation was a joke. I don't have time for this."

"Thanks for returning my call. How have you been?" Beverly asked.

"I'm fine."

"And I'm glad to hear that."

Silence.

Beverly dove in. "I didn't know that Macklin Hawk is your brother."

"Okay, Macklin Hawk is my brother. What about it?"

"He's agreed to be a guest on the Cherokee Show."

"Okay, he's agreed to be on your show. Is there something I'm missing, Beverly?"

"I'm just curious why you never mentioned it."

"Never mentioned it to who? You? And why is this any of your business anyway? I have a brother. News flash: I had a mother and a father too." The annoyance in her voice was clear.

"Sorry, Sandy. I was surprised, and I thought I'd reach out to you."

"Look, Bev, Macklin is an actor and enjoys being in the limelight. That's his life. I'm a doctor and I enjoy my privacy."

"I understand you're a gynecologist."

"GYN/OBI.

"Good to know. We need more women of color as gynecologist."

"I agree." Sandy said. "Is there anything else?"

"I've asked Erika Wallace to be a guest on my show."

"Erika Wallace?

"She's an attorney. Her father, Kenny Wallace, owns a multi-million-dollar investment and accounting firm which handles the Morgano Group's books. I'm surprised you've never heard of her.

"Oh, *that* Erika Wallace."

"Erika is pretty worked up about Jeremy. She recently visited Jeremy's Pub and found Jeremy in a compromising position with one of his waitresses. She had read my article on Jeremy and asked me to do a follow up."

"Let me guess. Since the Morgano Group is a client, Erika and/or her father's multi-million-dollar accounting firm can't risk exposing Jeremy. So, Erika wants you to do the dirty work."

"Jeremy's doing the *dirty work*."

"Okay, fair enough."

"Look, I just thought you should know, that's all."

"Thanks." Sandy hung up.

Jeremy was and still is a menace to society. Sandy would like nothing more than to bring him down. Shortly after the assault and rape, she found out she was pregnant and had an abortion. During the course of the procedure, she loss a lot of blood and developed an infection. Her fallopian tubes were removed; she will never be able to have children.

Sandy felt guilty about having an abortion and believed her

sterility was God's punishment. To *atone* for her sin, she went into gynecology. She's dedicated to making sure other women did not go through what she did. Her practice is a full service planned parenthood clinic. She treats women with insurance, as well as those who are unable to pay.

CHAPTER 15

Beverly was on her cell talking to Macklin.

"This is not an entirely unexpected call."

"Glad to hear that. I need to talk to you."

"When and where?"

"I'm free in between shoots today. Can you come by the studio around 1?"

"Sure."

"Thanks. I'll leave your name with security."

The security officer called Mack when Bev got to the studio.

"Please wait here, Ms. Andre. He'll be right over."

"Thank you." Before Beverly could complete a 360-degree turn around the studio, Macklin was at her side.

"Hey, Bev. Thanks for coming. You look great." Mack was sincere.

"Thanks." Bev was caught slightly off guard by his compliment. She was tempted to tell him how great *he* looked, but resisted the temptation.

"Would you like a tour?"

"Sure, why not."

The tour was short. The set was a police squad room with desks, chairs, computers, a suspect board, a holding cage, Mack's office, and wheelchair.

The tour ended at the cafeteria area. Mack opened the refrigerator and took out two bottles of water. He offered one to Bev and sat down.

"I'm not going to beat around the bush. I talked to Sandy. She told me she had given you some of the background information you used in your article about Jeremy Morgano's prostitution ring. She also said you're considering doing a follow up."

"I have considered it, but to be honest, I don't have anything new that might generate interest let alone an investigation."

"So, why did you call Sandy?"

"I called her because I learned you're her brother. Since you're considering coming on the show, I wanted to know if I could use it."

"A courtesy call?"

"Yea, I guess you could call it that. Can I?" She asked.

"Sandy told you about the rape, but she didn't tell she got pregnant as a result."

"And Jeremy Morgano is the father?"

Macklin gave her an exasperated look. "Whadda you think? Of course, Jeremy's the father."

"Sorry, but I had to ask. So, where's the child."

"Sandy terminated the pregnancy."

"Oh."

"The doctor who performed the procedure had an office that was one step up from the kitchen table. There were complications and as result, Sandy can't have children. That's part of the reason she's a GYN. It's her way of helping other women who can't afford good health care. As a matter of fact, she's treated a lot of the waitresses working at Jeremy's."

"Abortions?"

"I don't know. Patient/doctor confidentiality. However, Sandy has received death threats from pro-lifers. She's had to move her office twice."

"Which explains her need for privacy."

"Yes, it does, and I know this sounds selfish, but if it got out about Sandy being my sister, it could adversely affect my career. Sandy and I have agreed to keep our relationship private."

"Okay. You have my word; I won't say anything. However, I can't guarantee no one else will. The more famous you are, the more people dig."

Macklin nodded. "Ah yes, the price of fame. Thanks for listening. I hate to cut this short, but I need to get back on set. I'll walk you out."

"No problem. I understand."

"Beverly?" He was close enough to kiss her, which he was tempted to do.

"Yes?"

"This was business, but I really would love to get to know you. Perhaps we can have dinner?"

"I have a pretty busy schedule as I'm sure you do too."

"I'll make time. Deal?" He smiled and extended his hand.

"Deal." They shook hands.

Beverly was not sure if she was being punked, but she was flattered. The Hawk had asked her out.

CHAPTER 16

"Bev, come to my office when you get a chance." Rick was leaving a voicemail for Beverly.

"What's up, Rick?"

"Damn, girl, were you standing outside the door? He was startled.

Beverly laughed. "I was on my way to see you. So, what's up?"

"Good news, Macklin Hawk has agreed to do our show, and his *demands* surprisingly are reasonable, nothing over the top."

"Well, that's refreshing for a change."

"Yes, it is. Of course, he wants a guarantee that you will be doing the interview. No last minute substitutes. So, you better stay healthy." Rick admonished.

"I will." She assured him.

"By the way, he has a sister who went to the same college you did."

Ah shit.

"Sandra Hawkins. Name, ring a bell?" She felt Rick eyeballing her intently.

"Yes, Sandy, that what everyone called her, and I went to the same college."

"And, she worked at Jeremy's Pub, right? Was she one of your sources for the article?"

"Rick, you know better than to ask especially since you already know."

"What I don't know is why you didn't tell me that Macklin Hawk and Sandra Hawkins are brother and sister.

"I just found out myself."

119

"So, how do you plan to handle it?"

"I spoke to Macklin."

"When?" Rick's voice was getting tight.

"He called and asked me to meet him. I did and he asked me not to mention who his sister is."

"And what did you say?"

"I told him I wouldn't bring it up during the interview, however, I couldn't guarantee him that it wouldn't get out."

"Did you speak to his sister, too?"

Ah shit.

"Yes."

"And?"

"And she confirmed she's his sister."

"Don't be a smart ass, Bev."

"She's a doctor now and doesn't want the media attention."

"And did you tell her the same thing you told her brother?"

"Not in so many words." She knew she was giving him information in drips and drabs.

"Come on, Beverly. This is part of your job. We dig and we report on friends and enemies alike, as long as it's the truth. I hope you will do your job."

"I will. Is there anything else?"

"No."

Rick never believed that Macklin Hawk was Macklin Hawk's real name. Mack the Hawk wasn't a name. It was a brand; a TV persona. So, he had his people do some digging. He learned that Mack's *real* name was Macklin Hawkins, and that Macklin Hawkins had a sister, Dr. Sandra Hawkins. He then Goggled

Sandra Hawkins and learned she had attended Vantage College around the same time as Beverly had been a student. Rick pulled up Bev's article about prostitution rings and college students. The pieces began to fall into place. However, he wasn't interested in disclosing that Macklin Hawk had a sister. As far as he was concerned, it wasn't newsworthy at least not at the moment.

Beverly was curious. Rick obviously knew about her connection to Macklin's sister, Sandy, so, why the interrogation? She called Elliot Osbourne and asked him to meet her for a drink.

"Hi Beverly. Good to see you. It's been a while. You look great, as usual." Elliot kissed her cheek. "What's going on? You sounded so serious over the phone."

They ordered drinks and Beverly explained her dilemma.

"So, you want me to leak the story?" Elliot asked. "Of course, Rick will probably fire you for allowing another outlet to get a potential scoop. Have you considered that the story might not have much value? Mack, the Hawk has a sister, big deal."

"Yeah, I thought about that too, but I have a gut feeling that the story does have value."

"How so?"

"Sandy is a GYN and some of her patients are college students who also work at Jeremy's Pub."

"Abortion doc?"

"Macklin wouldn't confirm."

"Let me guess, doc/patient confidentiality."

"You got it. It's a planned parenthood clinic that dispenses women's contraception. She's gotten death threats and has had to move her office twice."

"Well, kiddo, whadda you gonna do? Elliot signaled the waiter for more drinks. "You got feelings for Macklin?"

"What makes you ask?"

"Oh, I don't know; call it a hunch."

"He's a nice guy. And he did ask me out."

"You sure it's real? I mean maybe he's..."

"Using me?"

"You're a good-looking woman, no doubt about that and you're smart."

"And I work for a news/social media outlet." Beverly finished his sentence.

"I'm sure having him on the show will generate a lot of buzz. Worse-case scenario his sister will be outed as an abortion doc and her office gets firebombed."

"Elliot!"

"Second worse-case scenario Rick fires you for not bringing it up."

"Win-win situation."

"When's the interview?"

"Tomorrow."

"Get a good night's sleep and trust your instincts. You're a good reporter, Beverly. I oughta know, I trained you." Elliot threw money on the table. "I gotta get back."

"I invited you. Put your money in your pocket."

"Call me tomorrow after the interview." He kissed the top of her head and left.

Beverly phone chimed alerting her she had messages. The questions for the interview had been forwarded. The questions regarding Macklin's background were innocuous. *So, Mack, where did you grow up? And what does your family think of having a super-star in the family?*

She breathed a sigh of relief. He could answer and she could let it drop. Rick might take issue, but he couldn't say she didn't do her job. She asked the questions.

The interview went smoothly.

Studio audience fans and groupies were outside the studio clamoring for The Mack's autograph and wanted to take selfies with him. Macklin was generous with his time. His security detail finally cleared the way for him to get to the limo. Mack the Hawk flashed a smile and waved to the crowd in true super-star fashion.

Beverly thought he winked at her, but she wasn't sure. *Just my imagination, running away with me.*

Rick interrupted her daydreaming. "You did good, Bev."

"Thanks."

"By the way, have you set up the interview with Erika Wallace and her father yet?"

"I'm working on it."

"Good, you might want to get on it right away."

Beverly had to laugh. That was Rick's leadership style. He asked the question first, and then he told you what to do. It was effective. She had her next assignment.

CHAPTER 17

Beverly called Erika later that day.

"Hello, Ms. Wallace, this is Bev Andre from Cherokee Media. How are you?

"I'm well, Ms. Andre, and you?

"I'm good, Ms. Wallace."

"Please call me Erika."

"The reason for my call, Erika is to find out whether you've given any more thought about you and your father being guests on the show."

"Yes, I have given it some thought. However, I will need more details before I can agree."

"No problem. I usually set up a meeting before taping so we can discuss details. If you give me some dates and times that are convenient for you and your father, I'll arrange it."

"Thanks. I'll check my schedule and talk to my father to see what's convenient."

"Works for me. Talk to you soon." Beverly said.

Erika very much wanted to do the interview. Her motivation was simple: she wanted Beverly Andre to do a follow up piece about Jeremy Morgano, hoping it might reopen the investigation into his prostitution ring. She was willing to do whatever she could to make that happen.

Erika had not talked to her father about appearing on the show and had no idea if he would be willing to do so. If he wasn't, she would resort to good old-fashioned blackmail. She'd tell him about the conversation she overheard in the bathroom in Washington, D.C.

As it turned out, it wasn't necessary. Kenny said he would be delighted to appear on the Rick Cherokee Show. His motivation was simple: he needed new business. Appearing the show was free publicity.

Erika called Beverly and told her she and father would be happy to be guests on the show. Erika agreed to provide background information prior to the taping. Beverly agreed to text Erika a list of questions.

On the day of interview, Rick sent the Cherokee limo to pick up Erika and Kenny. They were ushered into Rick's office.

"Hello." Rick extended his hand. He had debated with himself about whether or not he would remind Kenny they had met before, when and where. He decided not to mention it, at least for now. "Thanks for agreeing to come on my show. Please have a seat."

"Thanks for having us. I've followed your career and have been a fan for years." Kenny said. "This is my beautiful daughter Erika."

"Yes, of course. I heard a lot about you, Erika."

"You've heard a lot about me? I'm surprised." Erika responded.

"Correction, counsel, I've *read* a lot about you." Rick smiled. "Background research. Howard University degree in fine arts *and* a law degree. I'm impressed."

"Thank you."

"You're welcome. Can I offer you something drink? Coffee, tea, water, a glass of wine, if you prefer?"

"Erika?" Kenny asked.

"Water's fine, thank you."

"Coffee for me, Rick." Kenny said. "Black with two sugars."

"You got it." Rick served his guests personally.

"This is some layout, Rick. I understand you live here too." Kenny said.

Rick nodded. "Yes, I do and thanks. I'm going to have my staff set you guys up in the studio." He pushed a button under his desk which summoned his studio personnel.

"This is Raleigh and Evan. They are the best."

"I must warn you, the studio gets chilly." Evan said.

"Thanks for the warning." Kenny said.

"Please follow me this way. The studio is downstairs." Raleigh said. She was an attractive woman who looked to be in her early 20s. Erika looked at her father, who appeared not to have noticed Raleigh. But that didn't mean squat. Erika knew her father was a chameleon. She had watched him negotiate.

Beverly met them in the studio.

"Erika, it's good to see you."

"It's good to see you too, Bev." Erika said.

"And you must be the financial wiz, Mr. Kenny Wallace, Jr. It's a pleasure to meet you, sir." Beverly was all smiles.

"The pleasure is all mine, Ms. Andre and please, call me Kenny."

"Will do. And please, call me Bev. So, let's get this party started. I see you've been miked. Kenny, why don't you sit closest to me, and Erika please sit on the end. I'm sure you both know how this works, however, if you have any questions, feel free to ask."

Beverly opened the show and introduced her guests. She checked off Kenny's many accomplishments and successes as the CEO of a Black-owned investment and accounting firm. She then turned her attention to Erika. Everything was going well.

All three were comfortable, natural, and speaking freely. As the interview wound down, Beverly asked Kenny what advice he had for growing financial security.

"Thanks for asking, Bev, excellent question and one I get often. What I tell people is to invest in themselves. Put aside a little out of every paycheck, and don't be afraid to start small. $10, $20, $25, whatever. You'd be surprised how much you can accumulate. Another piece of advice: call me. (he laughed). I can help you build financial security, plan for the future and plan for your retirement."

"Well, that's good advice. Erika, what's on the horizon for you? You mentioned a theatrical project."

"Yes. I'm looking into purchasing a building in Harlem and converting it into a theater. There's a wealth of talent waiting to be tapped in the community. I would also like to thank you personally, Bev for the investigative piece you did on college students and prostitution. It is disgraceful how many of our young women and men are being exploited while trying to further their education. As you know, lots of students need to work to help pay for their education. Unfortunately, they are often hired by unscrupulous employers who exploit them. We need to expose those who take advantage of our students." Erika stated emphatically.

"Absolutely. I couldn't agree more. Thank you, Erika. Well, guys we're out of time. And thanks again to our guests." Beverly signed off. "Raleigh, make sure to remove the mikes.

"Yes, Ms. Andre." Raleigh removed Erika's mike first, then Kenny's. Erika kept an eye out to see if her father made any overtures toward Raleigh. He didn't.

"Wow," Beverly said. "I certainly didn't see that one coming. I'm the one who throws the curveballs."

"Sorry, but I meant what I said. From what I hear, the situation is getting worse. The problem is nobody talks about it let alone does anything about it."

"And who are you, Erika? The cape crusader?" Kenny asked. He was clearly annoyed with his daughter. "Don't think I don't know what you're trying to do."

"I'm not trying, Daddy, I'm doing, and I don't need your approval."

Rick came to the set and thanked his guests. "It's been a pleasure having both of you. The audience certainly enjoyed the show. Thanks for the money tips, Kenny. I'd like to talk to you about investments when you have time.

"By all means. Call my office and we'll set something up."

"Erika perhaps we can have dinner sometime? I'd like to hear more about your plans for a theater in Harlem." Rick asked.

"Sure. I'd like that." Erika smiled.

"How's Tuesday?

She checked her phone calendar, "Tuesday is fine."

"Great. I'll pick you up at 7. My driver will take you guys back. Thanks again."

Kenny Wallace and Erika Wallace rode back to the City in the Cherokee limo in silence.

CHAPTER 18

Rick called Erika and asked where she'd like to have dinner. She suggested Jeremy's Pub. He picked her up and they drove to upstate to the restaurant.

Mrs. Jeremy, formerly known as BJ, was at the Reservations Desk.

"Ms. Wallace, it's good to see you again. It's been a while."

"Yes, it has, and good to see you too."

"I see you and your friend have dinner reservations. That's so nice." BJ said. "I have a booth near the window with a great view. Is that okay?

"That will be fine, BJ." Erika said.

They got seated and the young woman Erika saw under Jeremy's desk brought them menus.

"Good evening, my name is Samantha, and I'll be your server tonight. Can I start you off with something to drink?" She asked.

"What's your pleasure, Erika?" Rick asked.

"They have some excellent wines. Are you familiar with Cavullo Wines?

"Yes, I am. Sauvignon Blanc or Rose?

"Sauvignon Blanc." Rick said.

"You got it." Samantha nodded.

Rick looked around the restaurant.

"It's different. Nice and kinda of cozy. It's got that college-town-restaurant vibe." Rick observed. "How do you know about it?"

"It's owned by the Morgano Group, one of our clients."

"We passed Vantage College. Are they clients too?"

Erika laughed. "No, the college is not a client. Are you familiar with Vantage College?"

"Only that it was founded by a million-dollar lottery winner." Rick said.

Mrs. Jeremy returned with their drinks. "Compliments of Jeremy's Pub. My husband sends his regrets that he is not able to personally greet you, Ms. Wallace."

"I'm sure he is. Tell him I said hi."

"I certainly will. Mr. Cherokee, my husband and I are big fan of yours."

"Thank you. That's always nice to hear."

"I can put in your dinner order, if you'd decided." BJ said.

"Think I'll try the meatballs and spaghetti." Ricks said.

"Shrimp scampi for me."

"Excellent choices. Enjoy." BJ scurried away, with her boobs swinging from side to side in synchronized fashion.

Word had spread to the wait staff that Rick Cherokee, the NBA player, was in the house. They surrounded Rick's table, asking for his autograph and selfies. He signed most of them before BJ stepped in.

"Okay, guys, let Mr. Cherokee enjoy his dinner. Back to work." She said with a smile. "Sorry for the intrusion, Mr. Cherokee."

"It's no problem."

Rick raised his glass. "A toast?"

"Why not, except I don't know what we're toasting to." Erika lifted her glass.

"To good company, conversation and hopefully, good food."

Samantha returned with their dinner. "Please enjoy."

"Thanks."

"I caught the show with you and your dad, Ms. Wallace. It was very informative."

"Why thank you Samantha."

"Please call me if you need anything". She smiled and started to walk away from their table.

"Everything looks good, and if you don't mind my asking what's your major?" Rick asked.

"My major?"

"Yes, I assume you're a student at Vantage. What year?"

"I'm a junior and a business major. I plan to go to law school when I graduate. Matter of fact, listening to Ms. Wallace reinforced my decision."

"Good to hear. The world needs more female attorneys."

"I couldn't agree with you more, Ms. Wallace. Women are wise arbiters and natural problem-solvers."

"Well said, Samantha and call me Erika. Here's my card. I'd be happy to talk to you. And good luck with your studies."

"Thank you. Enjoy your dinner." Samantha was obviously pleased.

"Um, this is good." Erika tastes the scampi.

"So is the spaghetti. I'd like to hear more about the theater in Harlem. Have you thought of a name for it?" Rick asked.

"Reparations."

"Hey, that's powerful. I like it. How long before you think you'll be ready to open?"

Erika laughed. "I have to buy it first."

"I'm not trying to get in your business, but if money is an issue, or becomes an issue, maybe I can help. I told your dad I wanted to talk to him about investments, but your project is right up my alley. I'd love to be involved with building cultural venues especially in Harlem, and I know a lot of people who might want to get on board as well."

"That's good to know. I'll get back to you when I have all the particulars."

"And you're good." Rick smiled.

Erika smiled sweetly. She was waiting for him to connect the dots. "What do you mean?"

"You've been leading me down a path a blind man could follow."

"You noticed, uh?

"Uh huh. Restaurant in a college town that hires students. Not to mention your comments on the show about college students and prostitution."

"Guilty as charged." Erika confessed.

"So, what's your plan? I assume you have one."

"I'm working on it."

"Alright then. Did you want dessert?"

"Thanks, but I'm gonna pass on dessert. But don't let me stop you."

He looked around and waved to Samantha. "Yes sir, what can I get you?"

"The check, please."

"No dessert? The apple pie is quite yummy." Samantha said with a wide grin.

"I'm sure it is. Maybe next time."

"Okay. I'm gonna hold you to that. I'll get your check."

Rick paid the check and left Samantha a generous tip. She ran to the door as they were leaving and thanked them for their generosity. "Ms. Wallace, I may be calling you soon. You guys have a great night."

On the ride home, Rick asked Erika more about her accusations of sexual exploitation of the waitresses at Jeremy's.

"Okay counselor, I know you had a reason for bringing me here."

"Yes, I did. I wanted you to see the enemy up close and personal, so to speak, even though you didn't meet Jeremy."

"Maybe things have changed."

"Wishful thinking. Things have not changed." She told Rick what she had recently witnessed in Jeremy's office. "I'm pretty sure it was Samantha who I saw running out of his office."

Rick's jaws tighten and his punched his fist in his hand. "That dirty son-of-bitch. That's disgusting. She's a young woman trying to get an education." Rick was infuriated. "What can I do? His ass belongs in jail; he needs to be big bubba's bitch."

"We need evidence; and we need the women to come forward. Otherwise, there's no case."

"How can we convince them come forward?"

"I don't know. They're scared and embarrassed. They're not going public. They don't want their parents to know, or anyone else for that matter, that they've been turning tricks to buy books. And even if they did, Jeremy will claim he didn't know his waitresses were having sex with the customers for money. He'll claim the restaurant has a strict policy against the workers *fraternizing* with the customers, but of course, he had no control over what they did on their own time."

"That's not acceptable, counselor. What about an undercover

sting? We can hire a young woman to apply for a waitress job and see if he hires her to serve more than food."

"Undercover stings take time and can be dangerous."

"Okay, okay, you're right. What about Samantha? She wants to go to law school. What if we do a show on college students? Let them talk about campus life, and having to work to defray living expenses, that sort of thing. Bring in alumni; do a contrast piece --- college life then and college life now."

"That's not a bad idea. We can get them together and have a discussion about their experiences. Talk to Beverly. She might have some ideas as well."

Rick laughed.

"What's so funny?"

"The way you switch hats. You took off your attorney hat and put on your theater art hat *and* now you're telling me how to run my show."

"Sorry, but Beverly can talk to Sandra Hawkins."

"How do you know about Sandra Hawkins?"

"I do Jeremy's books remember? She was on the payroll and she worked with Bev around the same time. Sandy, that's what everyone called her, left town suddenly. It was generally assumed she was pregnant. I also heard she was assaulted by a customer at one of Jeremy's private parties."

"She's also Macklin Hawk's sister. And she's a doctor now." Rick informed her.

"Get out! For real?" Erika was genuinely surprised.

"Yep. Mack told Bev before he appeared on the show. He also asked her not to mention anything about his sister."

"What's her specialty?" Erika asked.

"Gynecology. She has a family planning practice clinic in the City."

"That's interesting. I definitely have to talk to Bev."

They were in front of Erika's apartment. Rick got out and walked her to the door. The doorman greeted Erika.

"Good evening, Ms. Wallace."

"Evening, Jake."

"Rick Cherokee. What's up?" Jake extended his hand. "I've seen you play. You were good. Too bad you're not playing no more, they sure could use you."

"Thanks, Jake, that's always nice to hear."

"Say, Mr. Cherokee, would you mind signing this for my daughter? She plays on the girls' basketball team and swears she's WNBA material." Jake laughed and handed Rick a piece of paper.

"Sure, what's her name?"

"Jakequa Monroe. Sorry for the interruption, Ms. Wallace."

"No problem, Jake. Rick, I'll call you tomorrow."

Rick kissed her cheek and got into his limo. On the ride home, he made notes about how to expose Jeremy Morgano. He texted Beverly to meet with him first thing in the morning.

CHAPTER 19

The next day, Jeremy called his father and told him about Erika Wallace's visit and that BJ had seen her give Samantha her card. Jeremy had never told his father that Erika busted him with Samantha in his office the last time she was there to work on the books.

"Okay, maybe it's nothing. In the meantime, we need to do something about Lance Barrington. He's cut his Cavullo Wine order in half and I think he's dealing with another supplier." Arturo said.

"Or, he wants to renegotiate." Jeremy added.

"Yeah, well we don't renegotiate."

"The boy may need a reminder. He's getting a bit uppity."

The Morgano Group has been the supplier of wine and liquors to bars and restaurants in New York State for years. The Barrington was no exception. When Lance Barrington was first approached, he went along with the program. He was new to the restaurant business, but he wasn't naïve. He knew he was being overcharged, but things had gotten way out of control. Something needed to be done.

Lance Barrington never liked being bullied and he always had an ace up his sleeve. The Morgano Brothers (Jeremy and Billy) frequently patronized The Barrington. Lance knew Jeremy was a pimp and showed pictures of young women he was willing to make available to Lance's clientele for a price. Billy Morgano, Lance discovered, was a coke head. Lance hadn't yet decided how he would use this knowledge.

Jeremy had his marching orders. He planned to pay Lance a

visit, but first he needed to get more information from his wife regarding Erika's visit to the restaurant.

BJ was already at the restaurant when Jeremy got there.

"BJ, where's Samantha?" Jeremy asked.

"Probably in the locker room. Her shift just ended."

Jeremey headed to the locker room. He caught Samantha as she was leaving.

"Sam, can I talk to you for a minute?"

"Sure, Jeremy, what's up?"

"I understand you waited on Rick Cherokee and his guest last night."

"Yeah, I did." She moved toward door.

"You got what, another year in school?" Jeremy moved closer to her. "I hear things can get pretty expensive in the senior year, with graduation expenses. Plus, the fees for applying to law school, are pretty hefty too."

"Yes, it gets expensive." She nodded.

"You know I take good care of my people, don't you Sam? If you like, you can work extra shifts at the Pub, and I have a few private parties scheduled next week too."

"Thanks. I'll let you know tomorrow. That okay?"

He grabbed her face and squeezed. "Does your mama know what kind of waitress you really are? Does she know you're serving up your ass with the burgers?"

"You're hurting me." She tried to pull away.

"I know. Now, here's the deal, Sam, I don't want you talking to that lawyer. Understood?" He released his grip.

She nodded.

Lindsay, another waitress, was reporting for her shift. She was at the door of the locker room as Jeremy was leaving.

"Feeling better, Lindsay?" Jeremy asked.

"Yeah." She entered the locker room and saw Samantha's face was red and bruised. "Did that bastard do this to you?"

"Yeah, his bitch wife, *Mrs. Jeremy* probably told him I was talking to Erika Wallace."

"Who's Erika Wallace?"

"She's an attorney. She and Rick Cherokee had dinner here last night."

"Yeah, I heard there was a pro-baller here last night. And Jeremy's pissed off, why?

"Erika also does the books. She busted into Jeremy's office. I was under his desk, but she saw me as I ran out of the office.

"Under his desk?" Lindsay was puzzled. "What were you doing under his desk?"

"Lindsay!"

"Oh."

"She busted in before anything actually happened, but Jeremy's *thing* was hanging out of his pants. When he tried to zip up, it got caught in his zipper. He screamed so loud I thought it fell off."

"That must have been some sight and it serves his ass right. Hope he needed stitches."

"How are you doing? You were out for a few days. *Mrs. Jeremy* said you had the flu?"

"Flu, my ass. I caught an STD courtesy of one of Jeremy's friends. I went to an GYN who gave me an antibiotic. She's treated other girls working here too. I got the feeling she might have worked here before."

"I'm quitting this job. I've got less than a year of school and the tuition's paid."

"Can you afford to do that?" Lindsay asked.

"I've been saving to buy a new car, but that can wait."

"You think Jeremy's gonna let you quit just like that?"

"If he gives me a hard time, I'll talk to Erika. I'll tell her about the *private parties* and about the STDs we've all had. Jeremy is crooked as hell and I'd bet you dollars to donuts he isn't paying Uncle Sam either. This place could be shut down."

"Only problem is that *all* of us will be out of jobs and we *all* can't afford that." Lindsay stated emphatically.

"Erika's an attorney. She'll figure something out. Jeremy can't afford the publicity.

"I sure hope you know what the hell you're doing." Lindsay was shaking her head. "Jeremy *plays* rough. I heard he beat a waitress so bad one time that she had to leave school."

CHAPTER 20

Macklin Hawkins did wink at Beverly. He also sent her a dozen yellow roses in a crystal vase and a bottle of champagne. The card read *Roses are for Beauty; Champagne is for Class! Enjoy. Hope to see you soon and thanks. M.*

Beverly was trying hard not to twirl around, jump up and down and shout. *Mack the Hawk likes me.*

Rick walked into Beverly's office and saw the flowers. "Looks like somebody's got an admirer. Anyone I know?"

"Why, Rick, I think you're jealous." Beverly laughed and handed Rick a single rose. "Here. Don't say I never gave you anything."

"Cute and corny." He read the card. "I guess keeping secrets pays off. And I'm not jealous."

"I think you are." Beverly teased. "So, to what do I owe the privilege of this early morning soiree?"

"Erika Wallace and I had dinner last night at Jeremy's Pub."

"Are you serious? Whose idea was that?

"The dinner was my idea. I wanted to take her out as a thank you for doing the show. She suggested Jeremy's. Did Erika tell you what she saw the last time she went to the restaurant to update their books?

"Yeah. She said there was a young woman under Jeremy's desk, and his *meat*, her word, was hanging out."

"Well, that same young woman was our server last night. Her name is Samantha Evans, and she's a junior at Vantage."

"That's disgusting, Rick. We have got to do something." Beverly was angry.

"I want you to reach out to Samantha. Let her know you graduated from Vantage *and* worked at Jeremy's. Tell her we're doing a show about college students who also work to help pay their tuition and we'd like her to be a guest. Ask her if she knows other students who might be interested. Some of the kids working at the restaurant asked for my autograph. So, they obviously know who I am and might be amenable to being on the Rick Cherokee Show. As an incentive, we'll offer an all-expense paid weekend trip to the Big Apple. Put them up in a luxury hotel, wine and dine them. Give them a few dollars."

"Well, I see you've given this considerable thought. I agree Jeremy needs to be exposed, pardon the pun, and this time with his pants on. I just don't know if what you're proposing will work. Unless the women admit Jeremy is pimping them out, we've got nothing." Beverly stated.

"Perhaps, we can't do anything legally, but if what's he doing is made public, it could be bad for business." Rick countered.

"I'm willing to bet that the money he gets for his private parties isn't being reported to the IRS. I'll talk to Erika. Her father's accounting firm does Jeremy's books. If he can't be prosecuted, maybe he can be *persuaded* to put an end to the private parties."

"You think Mack's sister Dr. Hawkins might agree to being a guest on the show?"

"I doubt it. Jeremy threatened Sandy if she spoke to the authorities investigating the restaurant after my article was published."

"What!? You didn't tell me that. What else is going on, Bev?"

"Sandy worked at Jeremy's Pub as a waitress and then got *promoted* to hostess for Jeremy's private parties."

"Meaning she was having sex with the customers. She was a prostitute."

"Damn, Rick, it sounds so, so... what's the word, vulgar when you say it."

"Was she, or wasn't she, Bev?"

"That's not the point. And why is it always the woman who's vilified; who's labeled a prostitute; a whore? We should be focusing on the *customers* who pay to have sex with them. The *customer*, who is usually married with children, is never held accountable, seldom arrested, and they're just as culpable, if not more."

"You're right. And I agree they should be held accountable as well. So, what's the rest of the story?"

"The rest is confidential. What she shared is personal."

"You have my word, whatever she told you will remain confidential. I have no desire to damage her reputation."

"Sandy was working a party and a *customer* got too demanding and she refused to *service* the customer. The *customer* complained and Jeremy beat the crap out of Sandy before he raped her.

"Wow! Rick sat down.

"You damn right wow! Sandy didn't press charges, and few weeks later, she found out she was pregnant."

"What?!" He stood up.

"She had an abortion. The procedure was botched and now she can't have children."

Rick was quiet for a moment. "She's got to tell her story. I know it's painful, but it could help other young women who are being used as sex toys."

"Sandy is helping. She's a gynecologist and she runs a family planning clinic. According to Macklin, she's been targeted by pro-life groups and has had to move her office twice."

"Okay. Is there anything else I should know?" Rick asked.

"That's not enough?"

"I want you to get on this asap."

"Get on what, Rick?"

"The Rick Cherokee College Talk Show. You can change the name, if you like."

"I'm afraid to ask, but is there anything else you want me to do?"

"Yeah, thank your boyfriend for the flowers."

CHAPTER 21

Macklin called Beverly and invited her to dinner.

"I was just going to call and thank you for the beautiful roses and champagne."

"Well, we seem to be on the same cyber wave link. And, you're welcome. Are you free this evening?"

"Depends. What did you have in mind?"

"Dinner and drinks. Friends of mine have been telling me about The Barrington."

"The Barrington?"

"Have you been there?"

"No, but I've heard of it. The owner is some rich Jamaican with dubious credentials. Some say he's a Jamaican drug lord; others say he's a legitimate businessman and is being excoriated because he's Jamaican. Like there's no rich Jamaican businessmen who aren't drug lords." Beverly opined.

"Interesting and I suspect the truth lies somewhere in between. So, is 7, okay?

"7 is fine."

Macklin buzzed her intercom promptly at 7 o'clock.

"I'll be right down."

Macklin was standing on the curb next to the studio limo.

"Allow me." He opened the door for her.

"Thanks. It good to see you." Beverly said.

"It's good to see you too, Ms. Andre and you look great."

"Thanks." Beverly smiled and she felt her heart flutter.

Macklin was smoking hot, dressed in black slacks, black leather vest and a cobalt blue silk-shirt, with the sleeves rolled up to his elbows. They settled in the back seat, and Nick, his driver took off.

As they entered the restaurant, they saw Kenny Wallace talking to Lance Barrington.

"Isn't that Wallace?" Mack said to Beverly.

"Yes, I believe it is." Lance Barrington approached them as Kenny walked toward the back of the restaurant.

"Hello folks. I am Lance Barrington. Welcome to my establishment, Mack. Mine if I call you Mack? Lance smiled.

"Not at all."

"Great, Mack, and I'll have a bottle of wine sent to your table, on the house, of course."

"Thank you."

"And how are you, Ms. Andre?"

"I'm well. Have we met?"

"No, we haven't, however, I've seen your show." Lance answered. "Enjoy dinner. Evelyn will be your server this evening and will be right over."

"Thanks."

Evelyn, a young pretty woman bounced over to their table and handed Macklin the menu. She then rattled off the menu and her personal favorites. She smiled at Mack the entire time and never even looked at Beverly. When the *audition* was over, she took their order.

"If you're wondering why I haven't written anything down, don't worry. I'm a quick study. I've committed your order to memory, Mr. Hawk. Yours too." She said to Beverly as an afterthought. "Your dinner will be here shortly." Evelyn bounced off to the kitchen.

Beverly laughed. "She definitely a fan but I'm sure you're used to the star treatment. Must be nice."

"It is nice, but sometimes it's an inconvenience. Don't get me wrong, I am appreciative of my fans, but there are times when I like to eat in peace, especially when I'm with a beautiful woman—like I am tonight."

"Why thank you, sir." Bev smiled and battered her eyelashes.

Macklin laughed at her gesture. "You're welcome. And it seems you're no stranger to the *star treatment* either. You're on the air almost as much as I am. The ratings for the last few shows have been exceptional."

"That's because I had exceptional guests. You, and then the Wallaces—Erika and her father, Kenny."

"You did a good interview. Tell me something, was Erika Wallace's public service announcement planned?"

"No, it wasn't. It caught me off guard, although in retrospect, I should have seen it coming. Erika is determined to bring Jeremy down. Problem, of course there's a conflict."

"The Morgano Group is a Kenny Wallace Accounting client. She needs to find a back door, so to speak. Does she know about me and Sandy?" Macklin asked.

"If you're asking if I told her, the answer is no, but I can't say she doesn't know.

"I believe you, but I'm still worried about Sandy."

Jeremy Morgano approached their table. He tapped Beverly on the shoulder and winked.

"How you doing, Mack? Love the show." Jeremy waved at Mack.

"Thanks."

Beverly almost dropped her glass.

"Judging from your reaction, I take it you know who that is."

"Jeremy Morgano. In the flesh. You're pretty composed." Beverly drained her glass.

"I'm a good actor. Besides, what was I supposed to do? Jump up and kick the shit out of him?

"What the hell is he doing here? This can't be a coincidence."

"Probably not. I'm going to the men's room and then we're getting out of here. We can have dinner somewhere else."

Macklin spotted Evelyn and waved her over to their table.

"Can I get you anything, Mr. Hawk?

"Yes, the check. And which way is the men's room?"

"Sure, thing Mr. Hawk. Sorry you're not staying." She smiled flirtatiously. "The men's room is the second door on the right. I can show you where it is if you like."

Macklin thanked her and assured her he could find it himself. He walked to the bathroom and noticed Lance Barrington's orate name plate on his office door down the hall. Macklin texted Nick that they were leaving and to bring the car around. He walked into the men's room.

As Macklin opened the bathroom door to leave, he saw Jeremy and three other men heading toward Lance's office.

"What was that?" Billy stopped. "I thought I heard something."

"Check the bathroom." Jeremy said.

Macklin saw Billy pull out his pistol as he walked back toward the bathroom. Macklin ducked into one of the stalls. Fortunately, Billy was lazy. He looked under the first stall and left the bathroom.

"All clear." He yelled.

They burst into Lance's office. Lance was seated behind

his desk. Kenny Wallace was seated on the sofa. Both were smoking cigars and drinking brandy.

"What the hell do you want? I already told you I'm tired of being ripped off. I'm taking my business elsewhere." Lance knew instinctively this was not a friendly visit. He deftly slid his hand into a small compartment on the right side of the desk where he kept his gun.

"Yeah, well the conversation ain't over 'til I say it's over, capisce?" Jeremy drew his pistol.

Gerard (Lance's brother) emerged from a back room, gun in hand. Gerard put his gun to the back of Jeremy's head.

"Drop it, or I'll drop you." Gerard threatened.

Lance moved from behind the desk and kicked Jeremy in the groin. Jeremy screamed as he fell to his knees.

As Kenny tried to take cover Tommy Russo shot him in the buttocks. Kenny fell to the floor. His head struck the table rendering him unconsciousness.

Vic shot at Lance. He missed Lance, but shot Billy in the thigh. "Son-of-a-bitch, you shot me!" Billy yelled.

Lance looked at his brother, who was ready to shoot Jeremy. "No, Gerard, not here."

Jeremy scrambled to his feet. "Open the door, Tommy!"

Tommy opened the door at the very same moment Macklin tried to exit the bathroom. Tommy fired, hitting Macklin in the arm.

"I think I hit somebody. I'm goin check."

"No!" Jeremy yelled. "Billy's bleeding. We gotta get outta here."

The shots were heard throughout the restaurant. Somebody

screamed "gun shots!" The restaurant erupted into chaos as customers ran toward door, knocking over tables and chairs.

Nick, Macklin's driver, rushed into the restaurant. Beverly saw him and ran toward him.

"I heard gunshots. You okay?

Bev nodded.

"Where's Mack?"

"The bathroom." She was trying to remain calm.

"Get in the car. The door's unlocked. I'll find Mack." Nick headed toward the bathrooms. Beverly was right behind him. "Wait in the car." He shouted. "Call the studio. The numbers on the dashboard. NOW!

Beverly nodded.

Macklin had stumbled back into men's room looking for something to wrap his arm to stop the bleeding. All the towels were paper, so he used his vest.

Nick pulled out his gun and headed for the bathroom. He opened the door slowly and saw blood on the floor. Macklin was inside one of the stalls when he heard someone moving from stall to stall. He recognized the shoes; they belonged to Nick. Mack opened the stall door slowly. Nick was in front of the adjoining stall. He heard the door opening. He turned ready to fire, when he saw Mack.

"Don't shoot, Nick its me."

"Damn, Mack, that was close." He sighed and lowered his gun. "How'd you know it was me?"

"Your shoes."

"My shoes?"

"Gucci's. I recognized them in the dark. Where's Beverly?"

"Right here."

"I told you to wait in the car." Nick was perturbed.

"I heard you." She looked at Mack, who was holding his bleeding arm. "Oh my God, you've been shot. We've got to get you to the hospital."

"What the hell happened? Did you see the shooter?" Nick asked.

"More like shooters. I heard a few rounds and saw people running from an office in the back."

"Come on, we need to get the hell out of here. I'm sure the police are on the way." Nick said. "I'll call the studio from the limo."

"Fuck the studio. He's needs medical attention. Unless you want him to bleed to death in the studio's precious limo, we need to find the nearest hospital." Beverly was adamant.

They could hear the sirens of the police cars speeding toward the restaurant.

The police arrived and cordoned off Lance's office. They found Kenny Wallace laying behind the sofa unconscious. There was blood on the sofa, on a marble table, and on the floor. The police called for an ambulance. Lance identified Kenny for the police. He told them Kenny was an investment banker and a frequent guest.

Lance also told the police that three or four armed masked men had attempted to rob the restaurant. He and his brother Gerard tried to stop them, and during the course of the melee, a customer, Kenny Wallace was shot. He also informed them that both he and Gerard were licensed gun owners.

CHAPTER 22

Nick pulled off at the first exit ramp and called the studio.

"Jacobi Hospital is the nearest medical center. A rep will meet us there."

Macklin called Sandy. "Don't panic, Sis, but I've been shot," Mack closed his eyes; his phone slipped from his hand. Beverly picked it up: "Sandy, it's Bev. Meet us at Jacobi."

Sandy got to Jacobi and identified herself as a physician and as Macklin Hawkins' sister. She was told her brother was in surgery.

Beverly was being questioned by the police. When she saw Sandy, she pushed pass the officers. "Thank God, you're here. How is he? They won't tell me anything."

"He's in surgery."

"And you are?" One of the officers asked Sandy.

"Dr. Sandra Hawkins."

"And what's your relationship to the victim, Mr. Hawk?"

"Macklin Hawkins is my brother."

"Do you know how your brother got shot or who shot him, Dr. Hawkins?"

"No, officer, I don't."

"We'll be in touch if we have any more questions and tell the Hawk we enjoy his show." The officers walked away. That's it? Sandy was suspicious: was the shooting going to be investigated? She needed to talk to the studio rep.

"This is a nightmare." Beverly said.

Sandy sat down. "What happened?"

"Mack and I were having dinner at The Barrington. We

were just about to open the wine the owner had sent over, when Jeremy Morgano..."

"Jeremy!" She was definitely suspicious now and alarmed.

"Yes, Jeremy Morgano." Bev continued. "He came over to our table, claiming he was a fan of the show and wanted to say hi to Mack, he winked at me, and tapped me on the shoulder."

"So, he remembers you."

"Yeah, of course, he knows who I am. That didn't surprise me, but I got the impression he only knew Macklin from the show."

"You're probably right. Macklin never confronted Jeremy about what he did to me. He probably never made the connection."

"We decided to leave, but Mack had to use the men's room. The next thing I knew shots were being fired and all hell was breaking loose. Nick and I found Mack in the bathroom."

Beverly looked flush. Sandy was afraid she might faint. "You don't look so good. I'll ask one of the nurses to take a look at you."

"You think? Damn right I don't look so good. I just witnessed a shoot-out. Mack was almost killed."

Sandy is about to say something, when the surgeon approached.

"Dr. Hawkins, I'm Dr. Whitaker. I understand you're Macklin Hawkin's sister."

"Yes, I am. How is he?"

"Your brother sustained a gunshot wound to the upper extremity. We removed the bullet and there appears to be no damage to any major arteries. He literally dodged a bullet. He'll need to wear an immobilization device for several weeks.

Otherwise, he's fine. As you are no doubt aware, we must report all gunshot wounds to the police."

"Yes, I am aware of that."

"Your brother is in recovery. I can take you to him."

"Thank you. This his fiancé. We would both like to see him."

"Good, follow me."

His fiancé. Did she say his fiancé? Did I hear her right?

Sandy looked at Beverly, as if she had read her mind. "Close your mouth, Bev. You heard me right. Come on let's check on Mack."

Macklin was still under the effects of the anesthesia. Sandy called his name. "Hang in there, Mack. I'm right here with Bev. We love ya." Beverly squeezed his hand.

"You think he heard us? You think he's going to be alright? I'm scared, Sandy." Beverly said as they walked out of the recovery room.

The police questioned Macklin before he was released. He told the officers he had been shot as he tried to leave the men's room and he didn't get a good look at the shooter. They never asked him if the shooter was wearing a mask.

Macklin was wheeled out in a hospital wheelchair. Sandy and Beverly were by his side; the studio rep was standing in front of Mack. Nick opened the door to the limo. There was a swarm of reporters and cameras waiting outside. The hospital administrator read her prepared statement:

"Earlier tonight Macklin Hawkins, a/k/a Mack the Hawk, sustained a gunshot wound to his left arm. The bullet has been removed and Mr. Hawkins is being released."

"Was Mack shot during the course of a robbery at The Barrington Restaurant in Riverdale last night?" A reporter shouted.

The studio rep stepped forward: "The police are investigating and as such, it's an ongoing investigation and we're not at liberty to comment."

"Mack, how you feeling?" Another reporter shouted.

Mack smiled, "I'm doing fine, guys. Thanks for asking."

"Can you resume shooting with a busted arm?" Another reporter asked.

"I'm gonna try my best."

"Are the rumors true, Ms. Andre?" A reporter asked. "Are you and the Mack dating?"

Beverly was surprised by the reporter's question. Mack grabbed her hand. "Ms. Andre is a good friend." Mack smiled.

"So, Mack, who's the redhead?"

The studio rep stepped forward again. "That's enough for now, guys. Even Mack the Hawk needs to rest."

The studio rep and Nick got Macklin into the studio limo. Beverly and Sandy also got in and the limo sped off.

As they approached Mack's townhouse, Nick activated the cameras.

The studio rep was sitting next to Nick. "Dammit! Reporters are in front of the house."

"Mack, I think we might want to make a detour." Nick said.

Macklin was fast asleep.

"My house. 79th and West End" Beverly said.

"No, my house is better." Sandy said. "I have meds. First and 81st, Nick."

"You're an MD?" The studio rep was surprised. "And you're Mack's sister? I didn't even know Mack had a sister."

"Well, now you do and by now so does the rest of America knows." Beverly said.

They got to Sandy's house, and Nick helped Macklin to an oversized recliner in Sandy's living room.

"Is he okay here, or should he be in the bed?" Nick asked Sandy.

"Are you comfortable, Mack?" Sandy asked.

"Yeah, but I'm thirsty. I could use some water." He nodded.

Sandy got a bottle of water from the kitchen and gave it to him. "Sip it slowly."

Beverly checked her messages. Rick Cherokee had left several. She called him and brought him up to date. Rick asked to speak with Sandy.

"Sandy, Rick Cherokee would like to talk to you. Is it okay?" Sandy nodded.

"Rick, I'm putting you on speaker."

"Hello, Dr. Hawkins. Thanks for talking to me. First, how's your brother?"

"I'm good, Rick." Macklin answered from the recliner.

"Glad to hear that, bro. There are all kinds of weird stories flooding social media."

"Such as?"

"Such as you lost an arm; you're paralyzed and in a wheelchair for real as a result of a gunshot to your spine, which you sustained trying to stop a robbery at a high-stakes poker game at an upscale gentlemen's club in Riverdale, owned by an infamous Jamaican drug lord. Then there's also one about

159

a jealous girlfriend who shot you because you were cheating on her with Bev Andre, TV talk show host."

Beverly laughed. "You made that last one up, didn't you, Rick?"

"Sandy, would it be alright if I came by your place?" Rick asked.

"Sure." Macklin answered.

"He was talking to me, Mack." Sandy said with feigned annoyance. "It's fine, Rick. I live at..."

"I know where you live. I should be there in 30 minutes, and I'll bring reinforcements."

Sandy lived in a renovated factory building that had been converted into condo lofts. Rick was ringing her bell 30 minutes later carrying a large basket of assorted goodies and several bottles of wine.

Dr. Hawkins, I presume?" Rick Cherokee said.

Sandy laughed. "Yes, that would be me. Let me help you with these."

"Thanks for inviting me."

"I believe you invited yourself, but it's all good. How did you know where I live?"

"Research."

"Google?" Sandy wasn't surprised that Rick had referred to her as Dr. Hawkins. Beverly had kept her word about not disclosing that she and Macklin were related, nonetheless, it was inevitable that the information would be made public.

"Yep." He nodded. "Hey Mack, how you feeling?"

"I've been better." Macklin grimaced. "But I'm in good hands."

Sandy spread a bright red and yellow tablecloth across the

table and put out plates, forks and knives and glasses. She placed the basket of goodies and wine on the table.

"I would like to say grace. Growing up, our parents always said grace when we sat down to eat. You remember, Sandy?"

"I sure do."

Macklin blessed the food and thanked God for being alive and for the love and support of those sitting around the table.

Sandy got a corkscrew and tried to open a bottle of wine. Rick saw she was having difficulty. He put his hand on hers and helped her untwist the cork. It was subtle and sensual at the same time, which of course, was what he intended. Even though Sandy had on flats, she was almost as tall as Rick. She was wearing a navy-blue pantsuit and her red hair was pushed into a bun on the top of her head. The scent of her perfume made him smile. She looked good and she smelled good.

There was plenty conversation; everyone was trying to make sense of what had happened. The TV was on, and news reporters were dispensing the *facts* as they saw it.

Beverly had been watching Macklin. "Are you okay?"

"My arm hurts."

"You should probably take another pill and lay down." Sandy agreed and put him to bed. Before leaving the hospital, she had his pain medication prescription filled. She gave him a pill and within a matter of minutes Macklin was asleep. Beverly sat in a chair across from the bed. She was exhausted and struggled to keep her eyes open.

"Girl, get in the bed before you fall out of that chair and hurt yourself. I really don't need another patient at the moment."

Beverly laid down beside Macklin.

The studio rep was exhausted as well. He had been receiving

calls from the studio execs non-stop. Damage control was in overdrive. Rumors were circulating that their star had been shot at a drug and illegal gambling den. The studio's PR department also had been fielding questions from the press about when (or if) Mack would return. Finally, one of the execs asked how Macklin was feeling.

"He's fine, considering he got shot in the arm." The studio rep said. Nick has been listening to the studio rep. He was afraid the rep (intentionally or not) would tell them Macklin was at his sister's house. Nick knocked the phone from the rep's mouth.

"Whadda you do that for?"

"Don't tell them Mack is here." He hissed through clenched teeth. The rep nodded and picked up the phone. "What? I can't hear you. What? You're breaking up." He ended the call. "Now what?"

"Oh, my God! I forgot about Kenny Wallace." Beverly exclaimed as she ran from the bedroom. "I saw him at the restaurant talking to Lance Barrington. I have got to call Erika."

CHAPTER 23

Erika was at Paul's apartment in Harlem when Beverly called her. Beverly told her about the shooting at The Barrington and that she had seen her father at the restaurant.

"Did anyone get hurt? Erika asked.

"Mack was shot in the arm..."

"Oh my God. Is he alright?" Erika interrupted.

"Yes, we just left the hospital."

"Was my dad shot?" Erika's voice was shaky.

"I don't know." Beverly was struggling to remain calm. "All I know is I saw him talking to Lance and then Jeremy Morgano showed up. I didn't see him after that. Please call your father Erika and make sure he's alright."

"Alright. I'll get back to you."

"What the hell's going on?" Paul asked.

"That was Beverly Andre. She said there had been a shooting at some restaurant called The Barrington and Macklin got shot. She also said she saw my father talking to the owner, and Jeremy Morgano was there as well."

"You need to call Kenny."

"I am."

Paul anxiously watched as Erika called her father.

"He's not answering his phone."

"Call your mother. Maybe she's heard from him."

Erika called Renee.

"Oh, my Lord! No, I haven't heard from him. I know he plays cards at The Barrington, but he's never had any trouble there, as far as I know. Where are you?"

"I'm at Paul's, but I'm on my way home. Don't do anything until I get there, except call me if Daddy calls you."

Paul called a cab. "Car 133 in one minute and I'm coming with you."

"This is all my fault, Paul." Erika was in tears. "If I had just kept my big mouth shut about college students being exploited, this wouldn't have happened. Jeremy Morgano probably saw the interview I did on Bev's show. Even though I didn't mention the pub by name, he knew I was talking about him. And, now, coincidentally, there's a shooting at a club where he and my father just happened to be. That's no coincidence, and I will kill that son-of-bitch if anything has happened to my father."

"You can't blame yourself, Erika." Paul tried to reassure her, but his gut told him something was wrong. "Come on, the cab should be downstairs."

They got into the cab and she dialed her father's number again – no answer.

Paul put his arm around her. "We should check the area hospitals."

"Where's The Barrington?"

"Riverdale."

"You've been there?"

"Yes."

"With my father?"

"A few times. Kenny and the owner Lance Barrington went to school together."

"And what else do you know?" Erika's fear for her father had turned into anger towards Paul, as she moved away from his arm and looked at him.

"The Barrington is an upscale restaurant in Riverdale that caters to well-to-do businessman."

"It's an upscale whorehouse. That's what you mean, don't you?"

"No, that's not what I mean. It's an exclusive restaurant known for its gourmet food and whiskey, and high-stakes gambling."

"Served by barely legal young women, right? Gambling and half-naked young women. Two of father's favorite things. And yours too, apparently." Erika's voice was tight.

"No, it's not my *thing*."

Erika and Paul had been spending a lot of time together. In fact, up until this very moment, she thought she was in love with him. They recently had dinner with Renee and Lisa, who were both impressed with Paul. Renee was nonetheless cautious in her assessment.

> *"He's affable. He's got a great sense of humor and he's good-looking. All the attributes of a con man. Be careful."*

Erika was remembering that conversation as they stepped off the elevator to her penthouse apartment. Renee hugged her daughter.

"I'm worried, Mom."

"So, am I sweetheart. Hey, Paul thanks for coming."

"No problem. Have you heard anything?"

"No, we haven't." Lisa answered.

Erika's phone rang.

"Have you heard anything? Erika nodded. "Alright, we're leaving now."

"That was Beverly." Erika's hands were shaking as she put her phone on the table. "Daddy's been shot. He's at Jacobi."

Beverly had called Elliot Osbourne. She knew he had contacts in the New York City Police Department. His contacts confirmed the shooting and that Kenny had been taken to Jacobi Hospital.

Renee gasped. "Oh, my Lord, we've got to get to the hospital. Let me get my bag. Lisa, where are you parked?"

"In the underground garage." Lisa followed Renee to her bedroom.

Paul looked at Erika. "You've had a terrible shock. You want some water or something?"

"No."

Paul walked the terrace. He knew she needed her space to process the situation.

Erika joined him a moment later. She put her hand on his back.

"I'm sorry about what I said in the taxi, Paul. I didn't mean to accuse you of anything."

Paul pulled Erika toward him and kissed her passionately. "It's okay. I still love you."

"You, you loooove me?" She was stuttering.

Paul laughed. "Yes, Erika, I love you, even more when you stutter. Is it hereditary?"

"Yep, and there's no cure." She playfully punched his shoulder.

"Ma, Lisa, what's taking y'all so long? We need to get to the hospital." She yelled and walked inside.

"We're coming, dear." Renee said.

Renee's bedroom was visible from the terrace. Paul saw Lisa stroking Renee's back. Renee turned to Lisa and kissed her on the lips.

Ah shit! He had just professed his love to a woman whose father was addicted to porn, young girls and gambling, and whose mother apparently liked same-sex sex. He prayed it was not hereditary.

They all left the penthouse before hearing the breaking news:

> *"Kenny Wallace, Jr., owner and CEO of the Black-owned investment firm bearing his name, died late tonight as a result of gunshot wounds he sustained at The Barrington Restaurant. Details to follow."*

CHAPTER 24

Renee, Lisa, Paul, and Erika had gotten to the hospital 20 minutes after Kenny died. The surgeon told them Kenny had been shot in the buttocks. He had also sustained a deep laceration to his head and had lost a significant amount of blood. He went into cardiac arrest and died on the operating table. Renee was in shock. Her face was ashen.

"Oh baby, I'm so sorry." Lisa put her arms around Renee.

"No, no, there must be some mistake! He can't be dead" Erika screamed and nearly collapsed. Paul grabbed her.

Erika's screams broke through Renee's stupor. "Get her some water! We need a nurse."

A nurse took Erika's blood pressure. "It's high, which is understandable. She's had quite a shock. Let her sit here for a few minutes, and I'll check her pressure again."

"Mrs. Wallace?"

"Yes?"

"I'm Detective Dakota Johnson of the New York Police Department. I'm sorry for your loss, but I do need to ask you a few questions.

"Detective Johnson can this wait? My daughter almost passed out and her pressure has shot up; she may have to be hospitalized." Renee responded.

"I hope your daughter will be alright. I'm aware this is a difficult time, Mrs. Wallace, however, it appears your husband was shot during the course of a robbery, which is now, unfortunately a homicide. Anything you can tell me, may help. When did you last see your husband?"

This morning before he left for his office.

"Do you know why he was at the Barrington?"

"I know he plays cards there sometimes." Renee answered.

"Did he tell you he would be playing cards last night at the Barrington?"

"No, he didn't.

"Do you know if your husband had any enemies? Perhaps dissatisfied clients and/or employees?"

"That's enough for now, Detective." Erika had regained her composure. "My mother and I will be glad to answer your questions later. Right now, we need to make arrangements for my father.

"You're her attorney?"

"Yes, she is, detective." Renee answered.

"Very well. We can talk later. And, again, I am sorry for your loss."

Erika asked the nurse what they needed to do. She was told her mother would have to sign some papers and then make arrangements with a funeral director for the removal of her father's body. Renee signed the documents. Paul suspected the media might be waiting for them. He was right and hustled them out through a side exit. There were reporters outside the Wallace apartment as well. Lisa suggested they go to her apartment instead.

"Thanks, Lisa, but no." Erika said. "We need to be home." Erika had already called Jake Monroe the doorman at the building. He told her reporters were *all over the place*. Jake also told her he had arranged with the doorman from the next building to let them in through the service entrance. There was a walkway that connected the buildings.

"Don't you worry, Ms. Wallace, Jake got your back and my condolences to you and your mother."

"Thanks, Jake."

CHAPTER 25

"I'mma gonna kill that Jamaican muthafocker, his bodyguard, his motha, his fatha, his wife and children, his dog and his cat. His whole damn family." Billy Morgano was foaming at the mouth as Jeremy and the Russo brothers pushed him into the back seat of the car parked behind the restaurant.

"Where we going, boss? Vic Russo asked.

"Uncle Sal's."

Jeremy called his father Arturo and told him Billy had been shot and that they were headed to Uncle Sal's. Uncle Sal used to be Dr. Salvatore Morgano, Arturo Morgano's first cousin. Uncle Sal lost his license to practice medicine after being convicted of Medicaid fraud. With financing from the *Morgano Bank*, Uncle Sal opened a neighborhood butcher shop. He also patched up and/or stitched up family members and friends who wouldn't or couldn't go to the hospital where questions would be asked about how their injuries had been sustained.

Arturo Morgano met his sons at Uncle Sal's. Uncle Sal was stitching up his nephew Billy in a back room. Arturo was furious.

"I told you hotheads to *talk* to the Jamaican, not shoot up the whole damn place."

Tommy and Vic were watching T.V. in the butcher shop.

"Yo, Mr. M., you might wanna hear this. It's all over the news." Tommy Russo yelled.

Earlier tonight three armed masked men
attempted to rob Lance Barrington, the owner

of The Barrington Restaurant in Riverdale. Kenny Wallace, a well-known investment CEO was shot and killed. Mack The Hawk, star of the police action TV show was also shot. According to hospital officials at Jacobi, The Hawk has been released. Police are looking for the unidentified assailants. Anyone with information should call 911. All calls are confidential.

Arturo exploded. "You friggin idiots! Now the police will be looking for yous bozos."

"No, they won't. They said we had on masks, Mr. M." Vic stated proudly.

"You had on masks?" He asked.

"No, we didn't. Lance probably just told them that. He's dirty too. He doesn't want the cops snooping around his shit."

"He's no dummy." Arturo said.

"Sure, he is, Mr. M. He's Jamaican." Tommy Russo said.

"That's right. All dem Jamaicans is dummies." Vic Russo chimed in. They both laughed at their humor.

Jeremy was shaking his head. He knew his father was beyond pissed and that was dangerous.

"You need to do something about those two bozos."

"Take a walk, guys." Jeremy said.

"Off a pier." Arturo mumbled.

"Off a pier, that's a good one, Mr. M." Vic chuckled.

"We'll be right outside if you need us, boss." Tommy said. He and his brother high fived each other.

"I'll send them away until this thing blows over." Jeremy assured his father.

"I was thinking of something more permanent."

"I'll send them far away, Pops. I know they ain't the sharpest tools in the shed, but they're loyal. They won't snitch."

"For your sake, I hope you're right. I gonna make some calls and find out what the police know. You get dumb and dumber on a plane tonight."

"You got it, Pops."

Uncle Sal patched up Billy Morgano's leg, gave him a cane and painkillers. Billy convinced his father he would be fine at home and didn't need to stay at his father's house.

"Come on, Pops, I'll be fine. Uncle Sal patched up my leg good."

"It ain't your leg I'm worried about. It's your hot head. I want everyone, and I mean everyone, which includes you, to lay low. The police probably already know you and Billy and those a-hole brothers were at the restaurant when this Wallace guy got himself whacked."

"We went there to talk. I swear, Pops. The Jamaicans started the shit." Billy protested "That Wallace guy got shot in the ass by mistake."

"You being straight with me? The Wallace guy got whacked by mistake?

"Yeah." Billy answered.

"Well, mistake or no mistake, the Wallace guy's dead, and I don't give a damn who started the shit. You obviously did more than talk. And speaking of shit, you need to get off the powder. It's making you crazier than usual."

"Come on, Pops."

"Don't come on Pops, me. I may be getting old, but I ain't going blind."

"I know that Pops and trust me, I got everything under control. I just need to get home. Patty's due any day now and I should be with her."

"Home and hospital that's all. Is that clear?" Arturo was in his son's face.

"Sure thing, Pops. Home and hospital."

"Call me when Patty's ready. Another girl?"

"Nope. It's a boy this time, Pops. William Arturo Morgano."

"About time. Come on, I'll drive you home."

Arturo dropped Billy off at his home. Billy kissed his pregnant wife and said hi to his kids. He then called the Russo brothers and told them to pick him up from his house.

"What's up?"

"I'm running low." He made a sniffing gesture.

"Vic's got this new dude in the Bronx whose got some pretty good stuff."

"Great. You guys packing, right?" Billy asked.

"Is the Pope Catholic?"

"Here's the plan. We make a buy from your Bronx friend and then pay a visit to the Jamaicans. I got something for their asses." Billy laughed.

They drove to the Bronx and Billy re-upped. Mission accomplished, they headed for The Barrington.

They took the Major Deegan and exited at Van Cortlandt but failed to stop at the stop sign. A patrol car activated its sirens.

"Pull over now and exit the vehicle!" One of the officers ordered.

"What the fuck! We ain't even speeding."

"Stop the car." Billy yelled.

"What?!"

"Stop the friggin car." Billy repeated. "I'll handle this."

"We're dirty."

"Stop the car, Tommy. I'll handle the cops." Billy yelled.

"Ain't no way in hell I'm stopping." Tommy kept driving.

Billy used his good foot and stepped on the brake. The car jumped the curb, and hit a fire hydrant before coming to a stop. The driver's side airbag deployed, pinning Tommy to the steering wheel. Victor opened the back door and ran. Billy's good foot was caught under the brake, trapping him inside the vehicle. The officers drew their guns and ordered Billy and Tommy out of the vehicle. Billy untangled his foot and got out first. Tommy was unable to exit from the door, so he wriggled his way out through the window. Within moments, backup arrived; Billy Morgano and Tommy Russo were arrested.

Miraculously, Victor made his way back to Billy's house. Patty Morgano, being an experienced *mob wife,* took one look at him, and instantly knew that something was wrong. Victor called Jeremy. Jeremy called his father, Arturo who exploded. Arturo made some calls and learned Billy and Tommy were being held at the 22nd Precinct on possession of illegal weapons and drugs.

CHAPTER 26

Kenny Wallace was laid to rest a week after his death. His home-going service was attended by over a hundred friends and family. His father Kenny, Sr., in his rich baritone voice, delivered a beautiful tribute to his son in word and song. He held court in Kenny's den telling stories about his son to all those who stopped by the Wallace penthouse to pay their respects.

Marie Wallace kept a close eye on her granddaughter Erika. It was obvious to her that her granddaughter was taking her father's death hard. However, she felt there was something more going on. She sensed Erika was struggling with grief *and* anger.

The funeral and repast took a toll on Renee. After the last of the guests left, she was exhausted and went to her bedroom. Lisa followed her. Paul looked at Erika who appeared not to have noticed that Lisa followed Renee into the bedroom. Maybe she knows. Paul spent the night with Erika at the Wallace residence as well.

The next morning, they were sitting in the kitchen eating leftovers from the repast. Renee and Lisa went out to the terrace carrying a pitcher of mimosas.

"I need to go home to get a few things." Paul told Erika. "I should be back in a few hours. You need anything?"

"No, I'm good. I need to go through some of my father's papers. I know the lawyer has his Will, but I'm pretty sure there's a copy in of his office. I want to take a look at it."

"Is that legal?"

Erika laughed. "Yes, its legal."

"Well, he probably left everything to you and your mom."

"Probably."

"Okay, see you later, babe." He kissed her and pressed for the elevator.

"Wait a sec, Paul. I'll go down with you. I need to thank Jake for all his help."

Renee heard the elevator door close.

"Erika, baby, are you still here?" Renee called out.

No response.

"She's with Paul. They're outside probably waiting for a cab." Lisa could see them on street from the terrace.

"I just wish she'd told me she was leaving."

"She'll be fine. Come on, let's get in the jacuzzi."

Erika returned to the apartment and went to her father's office. She knew the combination to the wall safe and opened it. She found a copy of his Will, along with other documents pertaining to his various assets. There was an envelope marked 'desk combo.' She opened the envelope and there was a key inside. She closed the safe. Kenny's desk was enormous. She always joked with him about how big it was.

'This has got to be the biggest desk in America, Daddy. You got that much stuff?'

You'd be surprised how much stuff I got.'

Erika opened several of the drawers, however, the bottom drawer was locked. She inserted the key and opened the drawer. There was a leather case holding several CDs. She shuffled through them. They were all porn films. There were young girls on the cover in cheerleader outfits. Other covers depicted young woman performing various sex acts. There was one labeled *Kenny & The Cheerleader.* Erika felt like she had been punched in the gut. She threw them back into the drawer. There was another envelope labeled Renee and Lisa pics. Her hands were trembling as she opened the envelope.

Erika went to her parents' bedroom. She opened the door and saw her mother and Lisa in the bed together. Erika turned and ran.

Lisa saw Erika. Renee didn't, but she heard the door close.

"What was that?" Renee asked.

"Erika."

"Erika! She saw us?"

"Fraid so." Lisa shrugged nonchalantly.

Renee shot Lisa a look and jumped out of the bed.

"Erika, baby, wait! Let me explain." Renee was naked and crying. "Please, let me explain."

"Renee!" Lisa came out of the bedroom. She too was naked.

The door to the penthouse elevator opened and Paul was standing there.

"I, I, forgot my phone." He mumbled as he saw the two naked women and Erika standing in front of him. Paul was mortified.

"You can explain?!" Erika was screaming. "Explain these." She threw the pictures of Renee and Lisa on the floor. "Next you'll be telling me it's not what it looks like."

"I'm sorry, baby." Renee sobbed and crumbled to the floor.

Lisa picked up the pictures. "That son-of-bitch! Is this what that prick's been holding over your head, Renee? Is this why you wouldn't leave him? What did that pervert threaten to do?"

"Stop it. Lisa!" Renee yelled. "It's complicated."

"Complicated my ass. That pervert was having sex with teenage girls, addicted to porn and gambling."

"Paul, help me pack and get me the hell out of here." Erika said.

"Sure, babe. Come on."

Erika packed a few things. She opened her father's safe and took the copy of his Will and other papers. As she was closing the safe, she saw a small black-bound ledger. The ledger contained dates and money transfers from Albert Miller. There was also a note in her father's handwriting. "AM—$125,000—confronted him yesterday—told him to replace funds or I'm going to SEC and/or police – gave him a week. Tell Erika."

Kenny never told Erika, however, Albert Miller resigned two months before Kenny's death. His resignation sent shockwaves throughout the firm, and the rumor mill was in overdrive as to the reason. Erika was also surprised by Albert's sudden resignation. Albert had attended the funeral service and appeared to be overcome with grief. Aside from being a loyal employee for years, he and her father were friends. However, she now wondered if Albert's "grief" was actually relief.

CHAPTER 27

Because the attempted robbery of The Barrington was now a homicide, Detective Dakota Johnson was in charge of the case. She had joined the New York Police Department ten years ago and was now the lead homicide detective.

Det. Johnson had read the responding officers' report and had looked at the surveillance tapes of the restaurant parking lot. They were blurry but they did show the Morgano brothers (Jeremy and Billy) and the Russo brothers, Tommy and Victor, both of whom have long rap sheets for drug possession/sale and armed robbery, entering the restaurant. None of them were wearing a mask. She was also aware that Lance Barrington had been on the NYPD's radar for a while. He was a suspected drug dealer and had used drug money to open The Barrington.

She had spoken with the victim's widow Renee and his daughter, Erika at the hospital both of whom appeared to be distraught. She later learned that the woman with the clean-shaven head sitting next to Renee Wallace was Lisa Taylor, Renee Wallace's business partner. She had asked them a few questions and said she would keep them appraised as the investigation progressed.

Det. Johnson conducted interviews of the witnesses to the incident. According to Lance and Gerard Barrington, Kenny Wallace had been shot in Lance's office. Macklin Hawkins told the detective he was leaving the men's room when he saw two or three men with guns running down the hall. One of them shot at him. He ducked back into the bathroom and stayed there until his driver, Nicholas (Nick) Jones got to the bathroom and helped him to the car. He hadn't gotten a good look at the men, but he didn't think they were wearing masks. Beverly Andre basically corroborated Hawkins' version of events. Hawkins had gone to the bathroom. She heard shots being fired (she couldn't say how many). Nick Jones ran into the restaurant and she told him Hawkins was in the bathroom. Both she and Nick found Hawkins in the men's room. Macklin had been shot in the arm and was bleeding. They got him to limo and drove him to Jacobi Medical Center in the Bronx.

Both Andre and Hawkins acknowledged seeing Jeremy Morgano at the restaurant. In fact, he had spoken to Hawkins, telling him he liked his show. Neither of them was sure if they had seen Jeremy's brother, Billy Morgano, and neither had ever heard of Victor or Tommy Russo.

There was something about the way Beverly Andre reacted when asked about Jeremy Morgano. Det. Johnson pressed further, and Andre admitted she had worked at Jeremy Pub when she was in college.

That admission triggered the detective's memory. She remembered reading Beverly Andre's article about college students and prostitution which led to an investigation, but ultimately went nowhere. Nevertheless, she pulled the file. She had a hunch she could be on to something big and started connecting the dots:

- *Kenny Wallace, CEO of investment firm shot and killed during a robbery.*
- *Macklin Hawkins. TV star shot, but survives.*
- *Beverly Andre, journalist and talk show host having dinner with Hawkins; wrote scathing piece about*

college students and prostitution; Andre worked at Jeremy's Pub when she was a student.

- *Robbery attempt turned homicide at a restaurant that was running high-stakes poker games.*
- *Suspicion of drug dealing/selling.*
- *Jeremy Morgano and company at restaurant on night of shooting.*
- *Who was the intended target? Barrington, Wallace, Hawkins, Andre?*
- *Affluent/influential African Americans.*

Lance Barrington and his brother/bodyguard Gerard had also surrendered their weapons for testing. Ballistics were able to determine that the bullet removed from Kenny Wallace did not come from Lance's gun or from Gerard's. The detective suspected Lance and Gerard knew a lot more than they disclosed in their statements, but she needed proof.

She also knew that Billy Morgano and Tommy Russo were being held on weapons and drug possession charges. Their guns had been tested and ballistics confirmed both had recently been fired. Nonetheless, she was waiting for ballistics to confirm that Tommy Russo's gun had been used in the Wallace shooting. And, more importantly that Tommy Russo had fired the gun. If so, Tommy Russo could be facing felony murder.

There is a code of silence among thugs, but it extends only so far. When facing felony murder charges, it was not unusual for the suspect to cooperate with the police in exchange for lesser charges and less prison time. Said cooperation is usually contingent upon the suspect having something of value to offer in exchange. If Tommy Russo were to be convicted for the murder of Kenny Wallace, he could spend the rest of his life in prison ---- he was only 30 years old. Tommy Russo had incentive to cooperate.

Detective Dakota Johnson had attended the funeral services for Kenny Wallace. Kenny's widow, Renee Wallace, was distressed; however, it was obvious Erika Wallace, Kenny's daughter, was taking her father's death a lot harder than her mother. That didn't raise any red flags for Johnson. It was not surprising that Erika would take her father's death harder than her mother. Parents often shield their children from any unpleasantness in the marriage. Kenny Wallace and Erika Wallace were related by blood. Renee Wallace and Kenny Wallace were related by marriage.

Johnson paid her respects to both Renee and Erika. She noticed that Lisa Taylor stayed at Renee's side and they often grabbed each other's hand. She also noticed Erika Wallace's pure look of disgust every time she glanced their way. She had a hunch that Lisa Taylor and Renee Wallace were more than business partners. She knew there was a relationship, she just wasn't exactly sure what kind of relationship. Of course, she could speculate, but detectives don't speculate, they investigate.

Detective Johnson had looked into Kenny Wallace's finances, who at least on paper, was a wealthy man. She had contacted the attorney who had drawn up the Wallace pre-nup and Kenny's Will. She learned that Kenny's wife, Renee would not inherit any part of her husband's estate. It was unusual, but not uncommon. The attorney would only say they were other agreements in place which made it legitimate. Johnson asked about insurance. Renee was the beneficiaries on all of Kenny's life insurance policies. This of course could explain why Renee Wallace didn't contest her husband's Will. It also could be a motive for murder.

CHAPTER 28

It had been two months since Kenneth Wallace was laid to rest and the police still didn't know who killed him or why. The story had been pushed from the front page of the newspapers, but it was still news. Since Kenny had been CEO of an investment firm, there was speculation that a disgruntled client may have taken him out.

It had also been two months since Erika left the penthouse and had been staying with Paul. She was grieving, angry and felt betrayed by both her parents.

Her mother is a lesbian.

Her father was a sex-offender, who by sheer luck, had never been arrested. He was also addicted to pornography and gambling. It was sheer luck that the SEC hadn't investigated K. Wallace Investments. However, as Erika discovered, Kenny wasn't stealing from his clients. Except for that one $50,000 transfer from the Renee' Hair Care account to his personal account, there weren't any other questionable transactions.

In accordance with the terms of the pre-nup, if there was any sexual infidelity, Renee would not be entitled to any of her husband's assets.

Kenny also had taken out several life insurance policies and Renee was the beneficiary on all of them. Through inadvertence, oversight, or forgetfulness, he never changed his beneficiary on any of the insurance policies. Renee was still the beneficiary of a very large payout.

Except for charitable bequests, the rest and remainder of the Kenny Wallace estate was left to Erika, which included his shares in K. Wallace Investments, making Erika the major shareholder of the firm. The board also appointed her CEO. Erika was now a very wealthy woman.

Renee Wallace's financial future, however, was a different story and largely in her daughter's hands, who wasn't talking to her. Renee and Lisa were living in the penthouse. Because K. Wallace Investments had purchased the property, Erika was now calling the shots. By way of emails, she told Renee she could live in the penthouse, but not Lisa. In fact, the e-mail inferred Lisa couldn't even visit. This sparked a huge email war. Renee had been patient with Erika, realizing she was on an emotional rollercoaster, but enough, was enough. Lisa was livid: *'She can't dictate how you live your life. She needs to grow the fuck up and you need to get an attorney.'*

Lisa called Paul and they met at a tea café in the Village.

"I'm glad you called. And you look great as usual." Paul smiled. He hoped their meeting could lead to a reconciliation between Renee and Erika.

"Thanks, so do you, as usual." She smiled. There was a sensuousness to her voice. She looked at the menu. "I'm not much of a tea drinker, what would you recommend?"

"They have a wide assortment, however, green tea is always good for beginners." He ordered green tea for both of them.

The waiter brought a tray to their table with two cups, tea bags and a small teapot of hot water. "Let me." Paul poured their tea. "This mother/daughter feud has got to end. Things have gotten out of hand, especially about the penthouse."

"I agree. Lisa took a sip. "I'll be honest with you, Paul, I don't think Renee really wants to stay in the penthouse. She and I have more than enough to buy our own penthouse, two if we wanted. Erika is judging her mother, but not her father. We're all sinners, Paul, that's biblical and that's life. *'Let him who is without sin cast the first stone.'* Only Jesus was unblemished and without sin; not me, not you, not Renee, not Erika."

Paul nodded. "I've been trying to talk to Erika. She's grieving and she's in denial. Her perfect bubble of a world has burst. And despite her intellect, degrees and money, she doesn't know how to handle it. She's angry at Kenny, but he's dead, so she can't confront him. Renee has thus become the proverbial punching bag."

"And me." Lisa interjected.

"How's Renee dealing with all of this?" Kenny asked.

"She's hurt, Paul. She and Kenny were obviously living separate lives, but Renee she loves Erika. Kenny did too." Paul could hear the sadness in her voice.

"You're aware the police are still investigating Kenny's death?" Paul asked.

"Yes, I am." Lisa nodded. "Even though Kenny got killed during a robbery, the wife is still a prime suspect. Has Detective Johnson interviewed Erika?"

"Yes, she has. Not only is she Kenny's daughter, she's also CEO of the firm. Detective Johnson is trying to find out if Kenny had owed anyone money."

"So, what do you know about Lance Barrington?" Lisa asked.

"I went to his restaurant with Kenny a few times. The food was good and the high stakes poker games are a big draw. Kenny and Lance knew each other from middle school. Kenny was running a three-card Monte scam and Lance was the drug dealer."

"Lance knew Kenny from middle school?" Lisa was clearly surprised. Lance had never mentioned he and Kenny went to school together. She hoped Paul hadn't noticed her reaction.

Paul had always prided himself on his ability to read people. He suspected he had hit a nerve with Lisa.

"Do they serve anything stronger?"

"As matter of fact, they do. What would you like?"

"A shot of Henny."

He called the waiter and ordered two shots of Henny. Lisa took a sip.

"Better? He asked.

"Much."

"It's rumored that Lance is selling drugs from the restaurant as well."

"Is he?" Lisa asked.

"I don't know, but Kenny did set up an investment portfolio for him."

"Perfect way to launder drug and/or gambling money." Lisa observed. "Do you know how Kenny got those pictures of me and Renee?"

"No, I don't."

"Renee knew Kenny had security cameras installed in the penthouse, but he never told her about the cameras in their bedroom. Kenny routinely checked the cameras. That's how he got the pictures."

"You guys were stupid. Why fool around in the man's bed? I learned not to do that the hard way, but that's another story for another day."

"A story I'd love to hear on another day, but you're right, we were stupid. Anyhow, Renee discovered fifty-grand had been withdrawn from the Renee's Hair Care account. Renee knew Kenny had a gambling problem and figured he had stolen the money to pay off a debt. When she confronted him, he showed her the pictures of us. He had proof of her infidelity and according to their pre-nup, she gets nothing in the event of a divorce or his death."

"So, why didn't Kenny divorce Renee? He had the goods." Paul asked.

"Because Renee threatened to expose his gambling addiction. If his clients found out about his gambling, his reputation could be ruined. They might lose confidence in him; he could lose millions of dollars, not to mention the SEC would take a closer look at his business practices."

"So, they stayed married, each having something on the other. Now that's what I called wedded bliss. The Mexican Standoff has ended and Renee's still standing." Paul smiled.

"I suppose that's one way to look at it." Lisa nodded. She was thinking --- *damn, that smile's a killer.*

"I'll see if I can convince Erika to lighten up on her mother." Paul said.

"Thanks, Paul."

They left the tea café. Paul headed uptown. He was meeting Erika at the Harlem property along with the realtor and a City building inspector. If the building passed inspection, Erika would soon be the owner.

Lisa called Lance Barrington. "We need to talk."

CHAPTER 29

A month after being shot, Macklin Hawkins was back on set filming his TV series. The ratings had skyrocketed. The joke among producers and actors alike was that Mack needed to get shot more often.

Mack's social media fan club was full of theories as to who and why the well-known TV actor had been shot. Inevitably, the press learned that Mack the Hawk had a sister: Dr. Sandra Hawkins – the abortion doc. A pro-life organization tried unsuccessfully to close Sandy's clinic. They even suggested a boycott of Mack's show. The studio execs did not bend to the pressure, nor did the show's sponsors. Despite the short-lived campaign against Sandy, Macklin was concerned for her safety, and tried to persuade her to move her office for a third time. Sandy was adamant in her refusal to do so, however, she did increase security.

Rick Cherokee had been infatuated with Dr. Sandy Hawkins ever since he met her on the night of the shooting. Before leaving Sandy's apartment on that night, he asked if they could get together under less stressful circumstances. Sandy wasn't sure if he was sincere or if he just wanted to get laid. Nevertheless, she said okay.

They met for lunch the following week. Rick was interesting. Sandy always assumed that ball players, past or present, only talked about themselves. Rick didn't. In fact, he said about three sentences regarding his pro-ball career. After lunch, they walked through Central Park. They sat on a bench eating salty pretzels and talked. Sandy had a late patient appointment. Rick walked her to her office and asked when he could see her again. They had dinner a few nights later and a few nights after that. They took in a few Broadway shows and went to a basketball game at the Garden where they had courtside seats. Something was clearly happening between them and they both knew it.

Rick invited Sandy to his estate for the weekend. He showed her to her rooms which had a private bath, a sitting area, walk-in closets, and an office with a computer and printer.

He then took her on a tour, which included the Cherokee Media station, and the gym. When they got to the basketball court, Sandy put down her tote bag. She picked up a ball, shot a few hoops and made a few baskets.

"Beginner's luck."

"Really? How about a game?" She challenged.

"Sure, but you aren't exactly dressed for a game."

She pulled out a pair of shorts and a tee shirt from her bag.

"Always be prepared. Which way to the locker room? I presume there is one."

"Right this way." Rick showed her to the locker room.

She changed and wrapped her ponytail in a bun and returned to the court.

"Ready?"

Rick accepted the challenge and lost the game.

After the game, they went for a swim in the indoor pool and had lunch which Rick had cooked himself.

"It's an old Haitian dish my mother taught me how to make. My mother says a manly man helps in the kitchen and knows how to cook. So, I helped her in the kitchen and learned how to cook. Hope you like it."

"This is delicious. Your mother is a smart woman."

After they ate, Sandy told Rick she had to make a few quick calls. She didn't return for two hours. She was super-apologetic and hoped Rick would understand. She was wearing orange and black palazzo pants, a white gauzy blouse with bellowing sleeves which she had tied at her midriff. She was barefoot and her long red hair framed her face. Rick was completely smitten. They ate, drank and talked past midnight. They made love in front of living room fireplace. The next morning, they made love again in Rick's bed. By the end of the weekend, Rick, for the first time ever, was ready to commit body and soul to one woman.

Sandy knew how she felt about Rick and didn't want to deceive him. She prayed and asked God for guidance. They were enjoying dessert after dinner one night at Sandy's apartment when she told him about the private parties at Jeremy's Pub.

"There was this one guy who wanted a golden shower. I thought he wanted me to pee on him. I was wrong. He wanted to pee on me while I was on all fours. I told him that wasn't on the menu. I was trying to be funny, but he wasn't laughing, and he slapped me. I kicked him in the nuts and ran. The guy got to Jeremy and told him what happened before I could get to my car. Jeremy was furious. He punched me in the face, and I fell to the ground. He then kicked me in the stomach and dragged me by my hair to the storage shed where he raped me. When he finished, he spat on me, and told me I was fired. By the grace of God, I made it home and called Macklin."

Sandy was in tears. She told Rick she had gotten pregnant as a result of the rape and had had an abortion. The procedure was botched, and she could not have children.

Rick walked out of Sandy's apartment. He knew her story,

but for some reason, hearing it from *her* made him uneasy. The woman he was falling in love with had slept with men for money; had been beaten and raped; had an abortion and now could not have children.

He walked a few blocks and found himself standing in front of a church. Although Rick *grew up* in the church, he had not step foot in one in years. Yet, he knew intuitively that God had directed his steps and he was now standing in front of this church. He had an overwhelming need to go inside. He tried to open one of the doors, but it was locked. He rang the bell on the side of the door. He was about to walk away, when he heard the side door creak open. Two women were standing there. They told him the church was closed and that he should come back in the morning. *'It's Communion Sunday. We're setting up for the service at 10 a.m. Have a blessed evening, young man, one of them said.'*

Rick thanked them and returned to Sandy's apartment. Sandy opened the door and Rick embraced her tightly. Sandy had never shared what happened to her with anyone except Macklin and Beverly. Now, standing there with Rick holding her, tears flowed from her eyes. The floodgates had been opened. The pent-up rage and bottled-up anger she had suppressed for years came to the surface. Her feelings of guilt and her sinfulness were released. Rick told her he loved her and promised he would never leave her side again.

Later that evening, Rick told Sandy about his recent dinner with Erika Wallace at Jeremy's Pub, and what Erika had witnessed in Jeremy's office.

"And the server was the same young woman Erika saw in Jeremy's office? Sandy asked.

"In his office under his desk. You don't have to have much of an imagination to figure out what she was doing, or was about to do, if Erika hadn't barged in."

"He'd be dead if BJ had barged in." Sandy chuckled.

"Who's BJ?"

"Barbara Jean Morgano a/k/a *Mrs. Jeremy*".

"Ah, she must be the women who greeted us, but she never introduced herself and Erika never said who she was either."

"I'm just curious. How many dinners have you and Erika Wallace had?"

"Together?"

"Yes, Rick, together."

"And you're just curious, not jealous?"

"That's what I said, didn't I?" Sandy stood over Rick who was sitting on the couch. Her long legs look like twin towers. He laughed.

"What's so funny?"

"I'm picturing you with a scalpel in your hand. I suppose I should choose my words wisely."

"Good idea."

"Once. We had dinner together once."

"Good answer." She nodded and smiled.

Rick pulled her down onto the sofa, tousled her hair and started kissing her all over; he softly sang The Whispers classic: *Have you ever been kissed from head to toe; down your back, around your navel; well, you got that comin', my sweet and even more tricks and treats.*

"Yes, and please do the rest." Sandy whispered.

The next morning, Rick discussed his plans for a show on college students.

"Bev will reach out to Samantha. If we can get Samantha on board, she might be able to encourage other students."

"I like it. And if anyone can get people to talk, its Beverly." Sandy concurred.

"Speaking of talking. Are you sure you're ready?"

"Yes, I am. I meant what I said about going public. I have always encouraged my patients to go to the police, but I never did."

"What about Macklin?" Rick asked.

"I'll talk to him of course, but I don't think he'll have a problem with it."

"By the way, I think he's got the hots for Bev."

Sandy laughed. "The hots, Rick?"

"Yeah, the hots. You know what I'm saying?"

"Yeah, I know what you saying." She teased. "FYI, nobody says 'the hots' anymore. That's so old school. You feel me?"

"Feel this." He pulled her hand below his waist.

"Rick!"

"Okay, okay. I think they're dating."

"I know and if it means anything, I approve." Sandy said. "I think she's good for him. Bev is smart, strong and sensible. My brother is a gentle spirit. Of course, he's good looking, good looks run in the family, and he's a good actor."

"Does that run in the family too, good acting?"

"I said *he's* a good actor." Sandy sensed tension. "What's bugging you, Rick? Is that I had sex with men for money. Is that it?"

"No, well yes. I don't know. It's just hard for me to understand why you did it. I mean you were a pre-med student. So, you obviously had the academics." Rick got up and walked to the other side of the room. He was shirtless and had on shorts, which showed off his finely chiseled body.

"To be honest, Rick, I don't know the why of it either. I didn't take it seriously at first. The guys were old and always drunk. I did a few bumps and grinds, cooed in their ears, sat on their laps and it was all over. I never even took my clothes off."

Rick thought about how they both suffered near-death traumas that transformed their lives. Sandy had been brutally beaten and raped. As a result of a botched procedure, she cannot have children. He had suffered career-ending injuries and could no longer play basketball. They both survived and persevered. Sandy was now a doctor and he was the owner of a media empire.

"I'm sorry." Rick put his arms around her. "We definitely have to put an end to Jeremy's reign of terror."

"By any means necessary." Sandy said.

CHAPTER 30

Despite the passage of time, Sandy's hands still trembled as she parked her Mercedes in the lot designated for Jeremy's Pub customers. She said a silent pray and exited her car. She shuddered as she passed the storage shed where Jeremy had attacked her and entered the restaurant. For a moment she wished she had brought Rick with her, or at least had told someone where she was going.

"My God, Sandy Hawkins." BJ greeted her with open arms. "It is so good to see you. When I saw a reservation for Dr. Sandra Hawkins, I wasn't sure if the reservation for you, but apparently it is you." BJ's enormous boobs and Sandy's chest collided. "I have a table for one near the window."

"Thanks, BJ, however, I really came to talk with you. Can we go somewhere private?" Sandy said after she caught her breath.

"Sure, we can talk in the Club House."

Club House, you mean House of Horrors, Sandy was thinking. How naïve can she be? The Club House was a small soundproof cement structure connected to the restaurant via a passageway through the kitchen. There was also a door that allowed the private partygoers to enter and leave without being seen.

BJ unlocked the door and turned on a light. Sandy suddenly felt lightheaded and was breathing heavy.

"Are you okay? You want something to drink?" BJ asked.

"Some water." She sat down on a sofa. An ugly purple and grey sofa. She hadn't thought it would be this difficult. She was having flashbacks of her dancing on the laps of drunk, middle-aged married men who had daughters her age. She realized the trauma never went away. You simply found ways to handle it. She told her patients that all the time. Physician, heal thyself.

"Here you go." BJ handed her a bottle of water and sat in one of the club chairs. "So, what brings you by after all these years? I hear you're a doctor now. That's wonderful."

Sandy took a sip and got straight to the reason for her visit. "Yes, BJ, I'm a gynecologist. As a matter of fact, I've treated some of the young women who work here."

"Really? Who?"

"I can't disclose the names of my patients."

"Oh yes, that patient-doctor thing about privacy, right?" BJ nodded.

"That's right. However, what I can tell you is that many have contacted a STD..."

"You mean that stuff you can get if you don't wash or douche, or mess around with lots guys?" BJ shifted in her seat.

"STD stands for sexually transmitted disease."

BJ's back stiffened. "I know what it stands for. It's what you get when you have sex with a lot of guys."

"And, say for instance a husband has multiple sex partners and has sex with his wife, the wife could get infected with an STD or worse. The wife is only having sex with one guy, her husband."

"And you think my waitresses got a STD because they work here?"

"Because they worked the private parties right here in the Club House, as you call it."

"Is that what they told you?" BJ asked defensively.

"Pretty much."

"I don't believe you."

"I think you do, and I think you also know what goes on at the private parties. You have convinced yourself that as long as Jeremy wasn't participating, he wasn't cheating on you. Well, guess what BJ, Jeremy was and probably still does participate. He's had sex --- *unprotected sex* --- with most of his waitresses."

"I don't believe you. You're lying." BJ snatched the water bottle from Sandy's hand. "Get out!"

"You know I'm not lying, BJ, and you need to get yourself checked out. You could have a STD or worse." Sandy said calmly.

"You're a lying bitch! Is that what happened to you? Did you get a STD and leave school?" BJ was almost shouting.

"No, I left school because your husband beat the crap out of me because I refused to perform a sex act on one of his customers. He also threatened to kill me if I went to the police. You came to my dorm room. You saw what he did to me."

"Get out!" BJ screamed.

"He also raped me, BJ and I got pregnant."

"Get out!"

Sandy left. BJ called her father.

Barbara Jean (BJ) was Benito "Benny" Cavullo's only daughter. She was short and round, but she had a cute face which distracted from her peculiarly weird shape. Her enormous boobs shook when she laughed, talked, and walked. Jolly was the word many used to describe her. BJ was aware that people made fun of her.

The Cavullo family were wine and liquor distributors and

the Morgano family had been a customer for decades. About ten years ago, the Morgano Group became a distributor of Cavullo wines as well. As distributors, the Morganos overcharged its customers. Benito (Benny) Cavullo was aware of this but chose not to intercede. Both families were old school and marriages were often arranged. Thus, it was understood that Jeremy and BJ would wed. BJ was also the manager of Jeremy's Pub, which gave her stature. Marrying Jeremy gave BJ more stature. The wedding was huge and expensive. BJ floated down the aisle in a $25,000 gown, with a *how-you-like-me-now* smile on her face. She was large, round and most importantly, she would soon be Mrs. Barbara Jean Morgano. However, BJ was no fool, she knew it was an *arranged* marriage.

Shortly after they got married, Jeremy converted the back room of the Pub into a Club House, which he rented out for private parties. He asked some of the waitresses to serve as hostesses. Jeremy said it was opportunity for them to make extra cash. Rumors circulated that they were serving more than food and drink. BJ didn't approve, but as long as Jeremy wasn't having sex with any of them, it was none of her business.

Although it wasn't necessary, BJ continued working at the restaurant after she married Jeremy. It was partly out of habit and it also enabled her to keep her eye on her husband's wandering eye. She was killing two birds with one stone.

BJ became concerned when Sandy didn't show up for work and asked Jeremy what was going on. At first, he told her didn't know. BJ was persistent. Jeremy finally told her Sandy quit because she had been assaulted by a customer. BJ was alarmed. If Sandy had been assaulted by a customer, the restaurant might be sued. She found Sandy's address and went to see her.

BJ knocked several times before Sandy opened the door. BJ was aghast. Sandy was in bad shape. Her midsection was bandaged and there were bruises on her face. Sandy told BJ she had been assaulted. She didn't tell her she'd been raped, and she didn't mention Jeremy. BJ asked if there was anything she could do. Sandy said no there wasn't. BJ felt bad for Sandy. However, she was glad Sandy didn't say anything that would incriminate or be libelous against the restaurant.

That was the last time BJ had seen Sandy. She had also read Beverly Andre's (another former employee) magazine piece about the alleged prostitution going on at Jeremy's Pub. Her husband dismissed the article as being written by a former disgruntled employee, who was now working for a big-time magazine who needed a scandalous article to further her career. BJ never totally believed her husband. Now, she knew for sure, he had been lying to her.

CHAPTER 31

Erika was having a hard time containing herself. She and Paul were watching as the marquee, REPARATIONS THEATER, was being affixed to her recently purchased theater on 132nd Street in Harlem. She was beaming and hoped the grand opening would be within the next couple of months.

They celebrated at Paul's apartment. Erika was in a good mood, so Paul decided to bring up Renee and Lisa.

"I had tea with Lisa not too long ago."

"Whose idea was that?" The tone of her voice was not particularly encouraging.

"It was hers, but I thought and still think you and your mother have issues that need to be resolved."

"It's simple, Paul. I don't want Lisa living in my father's penthouse."

"Come on, Erika, what's the real issue?"

"The *real* issue is that my mother was cheating on my father. She totally disrespected him by hooking up with Lisa, her lesbian lover, in my father's bed."

"It was also your mother's bed. But it was stupid, and I am not condoning it. However, your father was also cheating on your mother with young women, some of whom were underage which, I might add is a crime and he knew it. He was addicted to porn and had a serious gambling problem. Yet, you're so willing to overlook his flaws, but so unwilling to do the same when it comes to your mother." Paul was trying to keep his voice even, but it was obvious he was annoyed.

"How is it that you know so much about my father's *'flaws'*?"

"Everybody knew, Erika. Your mother, Lisa, Lance Barrington."

"And apparently you knew as well."

"Yes, Erika, I knew. Your father wasn't exactly discreet. He and Giselle..."

"Giselle? Who's Giselle?"

"Giselle Garcia, the lead in the play. Your father was practically *touring* with the company. In fact, he was considered an *extra*. He and Giselle got together in every city where we performed." Paul said. The gloves had come off.

"Why didn't you tell me?" Erika was accusatory.

"Why? First of all, you're his daughter, not his wife. He was cheating on your mother, not you. Second, we weren't even seeing each then. And what would have been the point of telling you? And if I had told you, what would you have done? Have a temper tantrum? Demand that they cease and desist *or else*?

Erika's elation about her new theater slowly dissipated. Maybe Paul had a point. Maybe she was being unfair to her mother. She had to admit her father was far from a saint. She called her grandmother and told her she was coming by for a visit. Grandma Marie had a soothing demeanor, and always gave good advice, which was just what she needed.

CHAPTER 32

Detective Johnson was waiting for forensics to confirm that the bullet that killed Kenny Wallace had been fired from Tommy Russo's gun. At first blush, it appeared that Wallace wasn't the intended target. He, like Macklin Hawkins, was simply at the wrong place at the wrong time. However, it wasn't totally out of the realm of possibilities that Wallace was the target. Someone could have hired Tommy Russo to get rid of Wallace. There were a lot of loose ends that needed to be tied up. She had a gut feeling that Lance Barrington knew more than he let on during the first interview and decided to pay him another visit. Lisa Taylor was sitting in Lance's office when she arrived.

"Detective Johnson, how are you?" Lance greeted her cordially. "Can I offer you something to drink?"

"Thanks, but no."

"Of course, this is official business." Lance nodded and smiled.

"I have a few questions about the alleged robbery and homicide."

"By all means. I'm always willing to cooperate with the NYPD."

"Ms. Taylor." Detective Johnson addressed Lisa.

"Is my cousin." Lance responded before Lisa. "She was in the neighborhood and decided to pay me a visit."

"Detective." Lisa nodded.

"How is Mrs. Wallace? I understand you two are very close."

"Yes, detective, Renee and I are close and she's doing well under the circumstances."

"Just a few questions. Mr. Barrington. I believe you said the intruders wore masks. Is that correct?"

"Perhaps, I was mistaken, Detective."

"So, they weren't wearing masks?"

"Everything happened so fast, and I had been drinking." Lance answered.

"So, back to my original question: were they wearing masks?"

"As I've said, three or four men charged in here with guns. And sadly, my friend, Kenny, is no longer with us. I hope you find them soon so that justice can be done."

"Me, too."

"Ms. Taylor, would you mind if I spoke to Mr. Barrington in private?"

"Not at all. I was just leaving." She kissed Lance on the cheek. "I'll call you later."

"Okay, Detective, you have my full attention."

"Do you purchase your wines from the Morganos?

"Some."

"It's common knowledge that the Morganos have cornered the market, so to speak, and restaurants and bars that wish to remain in business, must do business with them at inflated prices." Johnson stated.

"It's a competitive business and I have been approached by many distributors, however, my arrangement with the Morganos is satisfactory."

"No strong-arm tactics?"

"That's not how I do business, Detective."

"Did Kenny Wallace owe you any money?"

"No, Detective, he didn't."

"Thanks for your time. I'll see myself out."

"You and Mr. Johnson should come by for dinner."

"Thanks. By the way, do you know if Mr. Wallace knew Jeremy Morgano?"

"No, I don't know."

Johnson had to give Lance his props. The man was as smooth as silk. The rumor was he has nineteen children. It was also rumored he has political aspirations.

Lance Barrington watched as Detective Johnson left the restaurant.

"Alright, the coast is clear."

Lisa had been waiting outside. She came back into office, walked to the bar and poured herself a shot of Hennessy. "What the hell was that about? You told me you had everything under control. And what's with the masked gunmen?"

"I told the detective I couldn't identify the gunmen because they were wearing mask. It was a delay tactic."

"Duh. I figured that out." Lisa swallowed her drink and poured another one.

"And who shot Kenny? You were supposed to *convince* him to give Renee a divorce, not kill him."

"I know what was *supposed* to happen. What I didn't know is that Jeremy and his crew...."

"Was his crew the Russo brothers?" Lisa asked.

"Yeah. You know 'em?"

"I know of them. So, Jeremy Morgano and his crew, were the 'masked' gunmen?"

"Yeah, I've been having a beef with the Morganos. They've been overcharging me, and I told Jeremy I wasn't doing business with him unless he lowered his prices. He didn't like that and decided to pay me a visit. Bullets started flying and Kenny got shot in the ass. Who knew a bullet in the ass would kill him?"

"Yeah, who knew? So, instead of divorcing him, she's burying him."

"Well, you wanted him out of her life. Now he is --- *permanently.*"

"Whoopee! The only problem is this Detective thinks Renee may be responsible. But I still don't get why you're protecting Jeremy?"

"I'm not, but I can't afford to have the police snooping around into my business affairs. I'll take care of Jeremy in due time, in my own way."

Lisa drains her glass. "TMI."

"You want Gerard to take you home?"

"Thanks, cuz, but it's not necessary. I'm good." Word to the wise, don't sleep the detective. She's smart and she's ambitious. Detective Johnson wants to be Commissioner Johnson, and perhaps she should be. However, she needs a high-profile case to get her there."

"And this could be her big break? Lance asked.

"Yeah. Think about it: Kenny Wallace, rich CEO of a financial firm dies as a result of being shot in your restaurant; Jeremy Morgano and crew, who have ties to the mob, were here that night; Macklin Hawkins, TV star, gets shot while dining with Beverly Andre, investigative journalist and talk show host. All on the same night."

"By the way, does Renee know that we're cousins?" Lance asked.

"No."

"Are you sure about that, or are you guessing?"

"I'm sure. And why didn't you tell me you knew Kenny from middle school?"

"It was long time ago and I didn't think it mattered." Lance answered.

"Well, it could matter to the detective. Be careful, cuz, that's all I'm saying."

"You, too, cuz." Lance kissed her cheek and walked her to the door. "I'll call you in a few days."

Gerard Barrington was waiting outside. He opened the car door and smiled. "Hey cuz, where to?"

"Thanks, but I need to walk off the Henny and clear my head."

Gerard raised an eyebrow. "You gonna walk to the Village?

Lisa laughed. "Yeah, right. I have a customer on 231st Street I've been meaning to drop in on. I'll have my driver pick me up from there."

"Be careful." Gerard closed the car door.

"Always."

Despite the many years Lisa and Renee had been together, she had shared very little about *her* family. As such, Renee wasn't aware that Lance Barrington and Lisa Taylor were cousins. Lisa wasn't joking when she told Renee she had a private investigator *tailing* Kenny, and the investigator was thorough. He learned of Kenny's relationship with Giselle Garcia, his fondness for underage girls, the escort services he'd used, as well as his gambling problem.

CHAPTER 33

Det. Dakota Johnson was also thorough. She circled back to the restaurant just as Lisa was coming out and followed her to a street-level hair salon on 231st Street. Johnson watched as Lisa and another woman (who Johnson later learned was the owner) greeted each other warmly. After about 15 minutes, Lisa left the salon. A car pulled up and she got in. Ten minutes later Callahan exited, and Lisa's vehicle took off.

CC Investigations was on the second floor in the same building where the hair salon was located. Det. Johnson ran a plate search on Lisa's vehicle and requested info on the hair salon. She sat in her car and watched as Carl Callahan entered the building. She gave him enough time to get to his office before ringing the bell to CC Investigations.

"Alright, alright." Carl Callahan shouted. He was holding his pistol at his side.

"Carl." Dakota yelled. "It's Dakota. Open the door."

"Dakota! Why didn't you say it was you?"

"I did, Carl. Now open the damn door and put your gun away."

Carl opened the door. "Dakota, how the hell are you?"

"I'm good. I'd hug you, but I don't want to get shot." Dakota laughed and pecked his cheek.

"Were you bird dogging me? I thought I saw the car."

"Yep."

Carl Callahan was a retired NYPD detective. When Dakota joined the force, there were many who still resented that a female of African ancestry was joining the New York City police force. Carl Callahan was one of them, but fortunately he wasn't as Neanderthal as some of his coworkers who believed women should be kept barefoot and pregnant. He didn't have a problem with women working, just not on the police force.

As a rookie, Dakota naturally caught all the rookie assignments, which she expected. It didn't bother her. She was eager and wanted to earn her stripes. She patrolled a 30-block span consisting of residential dwellings, supermarkets, clothing stores, churches and the local bank on foot and sometimes in a vehicle. She was friendly, and on a first-name basis with many of the residents and shop owners. She had developed a relationship with the bank manager, and in fact had opened a savings account at the branch.

It took less than two years for Officer Johnson to prove herself. She was on foot patrol when she heard drilling coming from an abandoned building next to the bank. She reported this to Callahan who told her it was probably *"just some junkies shooting up."* She didn't think junkies would be using hammers and drills. Needles, yes, hammers and drills, no. Her gut told her something was wrong.

One night when her shift was over, she decided to conduct a stake-out of her own. She saw two men enter the abandoned building and then she heard drilling. When the drilling stopped, she saw the men exit the building carrying canvas bags, which she assumed correctly were filled with cash. She identified herself as a police officer. She had already called for backup and the two men were apprehended at the scene. Her heroic efforts earned her the first of many commendations.

Carl Callahan started CC Investigations shortly after his retirement. During his police career, Callahan had procedural disagreements with the higher-ups and came close to being relieved of duty on more than one occasion. He knew he had gone as far as he was going to go, so he put in his retirement papers after 25 years. By that time Officer Johnson was Detective Johnson.

"Dakota! Come on in. What brings you to this neck of woods?"

"Can't an old friend visit an old friend? Dakota sat in one of the chairs across from his desk. A framed picture of Callahan in full regalia was mounted on the wall. "You're looking good Carl. How's the family?

"Family's good. Ryan's with the DA's office in Massachusetts, Susie just had baby number three and Betty's busy being the proud grandma. Here's a picture of the newest Callahan."

"She's adorable and she's definitely got the Callahan dimples." Dakota looked at the photo. "Glad everyone is doing well. How's business?"

"Not too bad, but I ain't in for the money that's for damn sure." Carl laughed. "It's more like a hobby, something to keep me busy. I ain't exactly the gardening type. So, is this business or pleasure?"

"A bit of both. I'm investigating the Barrington/Wallace shooting."

"And you're talking to me, why?"

"Why? Because Lance Barrington and Lisa Taylor are cousins and Lisa Taylor and the Wallace's widow, Renee are lovers. And because I think you were tailing Wallace at the request of Lisa Taylor."

"Assuming you're right, that means Lisa Taylor is a client

and you know I can't disclose anything beyond that. Not even to you."

"Yes, I know that. However, I think Lisa Taylor is connected to the Wallace murder, and I think she could be indicted as an accessory. When that happens, and I think it will, you could be compelled to disclose whatever your investigation turned up." Detective Johnson said.

"Let me see if I got this. You *think* Lisa Taylor hired me to tail Wallace. You *think* she's connected to the Wallace murder and you *think* she could be indicted. That's a lot of '*thinking*' going on. Dakota."

"It's what I do, Carl. You know that."

"Lisa Taylor is a friend."

"Is her cousin Lance a *friend* too?" The detective asked.

"In a manner of speaking. Years ago, Lisa Taylor owned a hair salon in Washington Heights. This was before your time. Anyway, she was having problems with break-ins. She asked her cousins Lance and Gerard Barrington to take care of the situation, which they did. However, their tactics led to several heads being cracked open, which led to several retaliations. Break-ins turned into bloodbaths. Lisa was very upset. All she wanted was to operate her business in peace. She then did something unheard of. She asked the police for help. The Barrington brothers surreptitiously provided intel that helped us to get the situation under control."

"And everyone lived happily ever after." Dakota concluded.

"Nothing like a fairy tale ending."

"So, what about Kenny Wallace? Did Lisa ask you to check him out?"

"Lisa suspected that Kenny was cheating on his wife, Renee."

"Lisa and Renee are lovers."

"Yea, I know." He nodded. "Seems these two gals have been getting it on for years."

"And you didn't find it strange that Lisa retained you?"

"Hey, I don't condone that lifestyle, but I'm an investigator, not a judge."

"I'm not talking about their lifestyle. Didn't you think it was odd that Lisa hired you and not Renee?"

"A little, maybe. But I got the impression that Lisa thought Kenny Wallace was using their *lifestyle* as leverage. Again, I'm not a shrink or a psychic. So, I told Lisa I'd see what was out there."

"And what was out there?"

"You know that's confidential, but let's just say, Wallace had some very bad habits. Now, that's all I got for you aside from a glass of Johnnie Walker." He reached into a side drawer and pulled out a bottle.

"Thanks, and I'll take a raincheck on Mr. Walker. Take care of yourself, Carl, and give Betty my best." She got up to leave.

"One other thing, Lisa also asked for some background info on Beverly Andre."

"Beverly Andre?"

"Yea, the nice-looking black gal on TV."

"Really? That's interesting." Dakota was genuinely surprised.

"I thought so too, and for what it's worth, I got the impression Lisa thinks Beverly Andre might be her daughter."

"She asked you to find her daughter?"

"That's not what I said. However, you're free to *think* whatever you like.

"Thanks, Carl. I'm glad I stopped by."

"Sure thing. Take care of yourself, Dakota. By the way, when you gonna get married and have some babies?"

"When I'm commissioner." Some things never change. Dakota thought to herself.

Dakota went back to her office. The tension she sensed between Erika and her mother and her mother's lover might shed some light on why Kenny Wallace was killed. And Lisa Taylor was becoming a major player in the investigation. If Beverly Andre was indeed Lisa Taylor's daughter, how did that impact the case? Did it have any significance?

CHAPTER 34

Billy Morgano and Tommy Russo were placed in separate interrogation rooms at the 22nd Precinct. They both asked for an attorney. As a result of the car accident, Billy's leg wound had opened and was bleeding.

"I need a doctor. I know my rights. You gotta get me a doctor." Billy rubbed his leg.

"And you also know how this works: you want a doctor and I want some answers. When did you get shot, Billy?" Detective Johnson asked.

Billy was in severe pain. "The same night we was at that Jamaican restaurant."

"The Barrington?"

"Yea, we was supposed to be having dinner and heard shots. We ran out and I guess I got shot.

"Who shot you?"

"I don't know. Probably one of those Jamaican bastards." Billy rubbed his leg again and grimaced in pain. "I need a doctor."

Detective Johnson called for an ambulance and Billy was transported to the hospital.

Arturo Morgano sent an attorney to the 22nd precinct to find out why his son was in custody and to do whatever was necessary to get him released. Jeremy reminded his father that Tommy Russo was also in custody and needed an attorney as well.

"That's his problem." Arturo was annoyed.

"It's *our* problem, Pops."

Arturo's cellphone rang. "Where'd they take him?" He asked and hung up. "Billy's in the hospital."

"And Tommy?"

"Why are you so frigging interested in Tommy?"

"Because either he or Billy shot Wallace. Plus, he knows a lot about the family business. We gotta protect him to make sure he don't blab."

"I told you to get rid of that dumb son-of-a-bitch and his idiot brother."

"Yeah, you did Pops, but now ain't the time for I told you so or playing favorites. We gotta get *both* of 'em out of jail."

Arturo called Billy's attorney and told him to find an attorney for Tommy Russo.

William "Billy" Morgano's wound was treated. He's released from the hospital, and both he and Thomas Russo are arraigned for weapons and drug possession. They were represented by separate counsel, pled not guilty, posted bail and released.

Detective Johnson had a hunch that there was a dispute between the Barrington brothers and the Morgano family and assigned an unmarked car to surveil the restaurant.

Victor Russo realized that for some reason, the police were not actively looking him. He also figured it was just a matter of time before his fate changed and before it did, he intended to *kill those Jamaican MFs*. Arturo strongly suggested that Victor take an all-expense paid trip to anywhere he liked. Victor had thus far declined. He told Arturo he needed to stay around to help his brother Tommy. Arturo was fed up with excuses, and finally made Vic an offer he couldn't refuse. For his safety and that of his family, Victor must leave the country. Vic's flight to Rome was scheduled to leave at midnight.

On his way to JFK, Victor stopped by The Barrington. Lance was standing near the bar. Vic entered and sprayed the bar with bullets. He missed Lance, but glass flew everywhere, liquor and wine spilled onto the floor. Vic fled and ran straight into the police officers who have been watching the restaurant. They ordered him to drop his weapon. Vic disobeyed the order and was shot dead by New York's finest. This was not the outcome that Arturo Morgano or Detective Johnson had foreseen, but as the saying goes, it was what it was.

Arturo wanted to get rid of Vic Russo, and now Vic was dead. However, he was afraid the Russos would retaliate. A war between the Barrington brothers and the Russos would be bad for business, which was the last thing he needed.

Detective Johnson wasn't a happy camper either. She, like Arturo, didn't want a blood war between the Barringtons and the Russos. She had hoped to flip Victor and/or Thomas Russo against the Morganos. Vic definitely couldn't be flipped now, and Tommy, who never had any love for the NYPD, was going to blame the NYPD for his brother's death.

Gerard and Lance were sitting in the office discussing how best to proceed. The Barrington shoot-out that was clearly meant to send a message.

Lance was only alive because Tommy Russo was a reckless gunman, rather than a skilled marksman.

"Man, we've got to do something. We can't let this go. Makes us look like punks and it's bad for business." Gerard stated emphatically.

"I hear you, Bro, but...,"

"But what? "It's eye-for-an-eye. Unless you got a better idea." Gerard was spitting mad.

"I had a conversation with that detective." Lance said.

"Detective Dakota?"

"Detective Johnson. Dakota is her first name." Lance corrected him.

"Whatever."

"I get the impression she wants the Morganos as much as we do."

"Interesting." Gerard said.

"Yes, it is. I say we let her do the heavy lifting."

"That way we can keep our hands clean."

"Exactly." Lance nodded.

CHAPTER 35

BJ was still reeling from her conversation with Sandy. Deep down, she knew Sandy wasn't lying and she wasn't that surprised to learn that Jeremy had been cheating on her. All she ever wanted was to marry Jeremy and have his babies. Her own insecurities led her to believe it was her fault she was childless. She thought that being overweight made her infertile. Of course, no doctor ever said that, but it was suggested that if she lost weight, it might be easier for her to conceive. She had spent a fortune on diet plans and pills. Jeremy never complained about her weight, and he still made love to her. So, as far as she was concerned, things were okay between them. She now realized *things* had never been okay. She finally understood why Jeremy never complained about her weight or her inability to conceive. It was easy for him to act like he cared, or dare she think, loved her. She was no more than a business transaction. He was cheating on her with the waitresses who worked at the Pub. The very same waitresses she worked with. She could just imagine what they were saying behind her back. The fat jokes were bad enough, but this was unbearable. She was humiliated. The thought that Sandy was the mother of her husband's child seared a hole in her heart. Who else knew about her husband's bastard child. How many children did her husband have? How many women had he raped?

BJ and Jeremy had recently celebrated another wedding anniversary. As was his custom, Jeremy bought BJ an expensive piece of jewelry. This year it was a stunning five-carat diamond and sapphire broach, and they had been more intimate than usual.

BJ made an appointment with her gynecologist, who confirmed that she had a STD and gave her a prescription. She also gave her a prescription for Jeremy. BJ filled her prescription and then went to see her father, Benito (Benny) Cavullo and her brothers. She told them that Jeremy had raped and fathered a child with a former waitress. Her father and brothers weren't surprised. They were aware of the private parties and thought Jeremy was an uncouth, uneducated, disgusting pig. Nonetheless, BJ loved him, so they were civil toward Jeremy. However, should Jeremy ever mistreat BJ, there would be hell to pay.

BJ and her brothers drove to the Pub in the family truck. Because it was Monday, Jeremy Pub's was closed. BJ disabled the alarm and they went directly to Jeremy's office.

"I want the Club House destroyed; from the ceiling to the floor, every stick of furniture." She threw a set of keys to one of her brothers.

"There are hammers and crowbars in the storage room. Bring whatever you can carry. The rooms in the back are where the private parties are held. I want that place demolished."

Her brothers started breaking up the bar, barstools, tables, and chairs. BJ used a crowbar to rip the cushions on the four sofas on the back and side walls, and the green felt off the pool tables.

When they finished busting up the place, BJ sent an email to the entire staff advising them that they had been fired, however, severance pay had been deposited into their direct deposit accounts.

She reset the silent alarm which alerted Jeremy. He arrived at the restaurant within minutes and went directly to his office where BJ was seated at his desk.

"What the hell happened? Did someone break in?" Jeremy was sweating.

"I did."

"What the fu...?"

She got up and was in his face. "And I fired the staff, sent them a $1000 severance pay and your little pleasure dome has been destroyed. Go, take a look."

He pushed past her and ran to the room in the back. He saw the damage and ran back to his office.

"You fat bitch! I gonna beat the shit out of your fat ass." He yelled and approached BJ.

Her brothers were on him before he could even raise his hand.

"No, brother-in-law, we're gonna beat the shit out of your punk ass."

"What the hell!" Jeremy was stunned. He hadn't even seen them. He tried to run. The Cavullo brothers grabbed him by his hair. The beat down was vicious. Jeremy was laying on the floor bloody, bruised and semi-conscious.

BJ threw the doctor's prescription on his bloody chest.

Tommy Russo and the Russo family were devastated by Victor's death and wanted revenge. Tommy called Arturo Morgano and requested a sit-down.

"I know the cops killed Vic, but I want those Jamaicans

bastards to pay, and I want you guys to take care of it." Tommy was emphatic.

"You're talking out your ass, Tommy." Jeremy waved his hand dismissively.

"No, I'm not. I've been loyal and you guys owe me."

"And you've been richly rewarded for your loyalty. I made you and Vic millionaire punks. And I told you and Vic I would handle the situation. But Vic didn't listen and now he's dead." Arturo said.

"Are you saying Vic got what he deserved?"

"I'm saying if Vic had left the country, he'd still be alive." Arturo answered.

"You know he's right, Tommy. I'm sorry Vic is gone, but in a way, it was his own fault. He should have listened." Jeremy concurred with his father.

"So, the answer's no. You guys ain't gonna help me get those bastards? Tommy's face was red.

"Yea, the answer's no." Arturo stood.

One of the Assistant DAs contacted Detective Johnson and told her Tommy Russo had information about the Wallace shooting and was ready to talk.

"Just the Wallace shooting?" Det. Johnson inquired.

"You and I both know the man knows a lot more, but it's a start. Give me a rundown on what you suspect he might know, and I'll take it from there."

"You got it." This was the break she was hoping for. She requisitioned the file on the Morganos from the police file room. However, she already knew from past experience that requisitioning a file was just step one in the process. If she wanted the file copied, she would have to fill out a 'copy request" --- step two. To speed up the process, she did what all good detectives do and took the file to an outside (unauthorized) copy service. It was quicker, but not without complications. The clerk at the copy service was related to the Morgano family. He spotted the Morgano name and called Jeremy.

Jeremy was at his father's house when the clerk called. Jeremy told him to make an extra copy. One of his guys had already told him about seeing Tommy Russo at the DA's office.

"That son of bitch is going to talk!" Jeremy exploded.

"So much for him not being a snitch." Arturo said matter-of-factly.

"I could kill him with my bare hands. We've been good to him and his family. Vic was a hothead and he got hisself killed." Jeremy pounded on the table forgetting his hands are still bandaged as a result of the beat-down from BJ's brothers. He grimaced. "Ow."

"Call Philly." Arturo said. "You won't be killing anyone with your bare hands until they heal."

"Good idea."

"And, make sure you use a throw-away phone."

"Maybe I should have somebody else call."

"No, you do it. We don't need nobody else involved."

"You're right, as usual. Consider it done, Pops."

Philly Hudson slipped into town the day after receiving Jeremy's call and followed Tommy Russo for a week. Tommy and his side-chick had been hooking up at a motel near the

Verrazano Bridge. It was dark when they left the motel. They enjoyed a passionate kiss. The side-chick got into her car and drove off. Tommy walked to his car. Always mob-vigilant, he looked around before entering his car. For a split second, he thought he saw someone moving toward him. He stopped and looked again. Nothing. As he got closer to his car, he took another look around. Nothing. He got in. Before Tommy could start his engine, he was shot dead.

Philly returned the rental car at the airport and boarded a plane.

Early the next morning, the motel clerk discovered Tommy Russo's body slumped over the steering wheel of his car and called the police.

Detective Johnson had the Barrington brothers brought in for questioning. Both had alibis which checked out.

Det. Johnson suspected Russo's murder was a hit ordered by the Morganos. She paid Callahan another visit and told him what she suspected. Callahan concurred with her assessment of the situation. He also told her Arturo Morgano always used out of town talent. Most recently, the name Philly Hudson had popped up.

Callahan added, *"I figura Philly is a nickname, so there's probably no record in the database."*

She checked the database for variations of the name Philly.

The drug and weapons charges against Billy Morgano would probably result in less than a year jail time, if that. Forensics had finally confirmed Tommy Russo fired the gun that killed Kenny Wallace, and now Tommy was dead. And thanks to the NYPD, so was Victor Russo, one of the alleged *masked* gun men who tried to rob The Barrington.

Tommy Russo's mob-style execution made the headlines, as did his brother, Victor Russo's death courtesy of the NYPD. The police had linked the late Russo brothers to the Morgano family, and their alleged mob ties.

CHAPTER 36

Sandy, Beverly, Paul, and Macklin were sitting in Rick's living room. He had set up a storyboard detailing what he considered the pertinent facts. And, as usual, he had laid out a lavish spread of food goodies and beverages.

"As you can see," Rick pointed to the storyboard, "aside from the basics, this doesn't tell us much and we're going to need more to bring Jeremy down. However, in light of the police investigation into the Russo killings, the Morgano family has been drawn into the mix. This development might be helpful."

Beverly had reached out to Samantha, who agreed to appear on his show, but only *after* she graduated --- *a year from now*. Sandy was willing to go public, but her story was just that, her story and it was an old story. Rick needed something more. Plus, he had fallen in love with Sandy and the possibility of her being harmed in any way was totally unacceptable.

"I'm not comfortable with Sandy telling her story." Macklin frowned. "I think the police investigation into the shootings at the Barrington will ultimately prove to be more productive. Detective Johnson knows Jeremy was at the restaurant. I saw him and his pals going into Lance Barrington's office and then I heard shots. I don't think that was a coincidence. Of course, I didn't see who shot Wallace..."

"Or who shot you for that matter." Sandy interjected.

"True, but I still believe the detective is the best person to build a case against Jeremy, and she's got the manpower."

"Mack's got a point. It's no secret that the Morganos have ties to organized crime. We need to find out if Lance Barrington was being strong-armed to buy his liquors from the Morganos exclusively. Jeremy and Lance could be feuding over their arrangement." Beverly added.

"Which would also explain Jeremy and his boys busting into Lance's office guns blazing." Rick said with enthusiasm.

"Since I'm a victim, I'm going to demand that the police department find out who shot me." Macklin said.

"And there's nothing like a little celebrity to shake things up." Beverly interjected.

"Little celebrity? According to social media and my fans, I am huge."

"Oops, sorry, did I say *little*? What the hell was I thinking?" Beverly slapped her hand against her forehead. "I meant *huge* celebrity on the most popular show on TV *ev....vah!*

They all laughed.

"Okay, okay, I guess I deserved that." Macklin pulled Beverly toward him and kissed her on the cheek.

"Yes, you did." She teased and pinched his butt.

"I saw that." Sandy said.

"We all saw that. Damn girl, control yourself." Rick shook his head and grinned.

"Where's the fun in that?" Beverly pinched Mack's butt again.

"Oooh, baby."

"Um, can we get back to business? Rick inquired.

"Guys, there's something I need to tell you. I went to see BJ Morgano and told her about Jeremy." Sandy braced herself for their reactions.

"You did what?! Rick exclaimed. "You told that woman her husband had raped you?"

"And got me pregnant." Sandy added. "I also told her she should get herself tested for an STD."

"Let me guess. If she tested positive for an STD, you were hoping she'd drop a dime on Jeremy's illegal enterprise." Macklin asked.

"She might cut off his balls, but I don't see her going to the police." Beverly observed. "Did she ask you what happened to the baby?"

"No, she didn't."

"And you didn't tell her?" Beverly asked.

"No, I didn't."

"So, she's thinking you had her husband's baby." Beverly laughed. "That's precious. That oughta get her Guinea, sorry Italian blood boiling. Maybe she will cut off his balls."

"Exactly." Sandy said.

"Guinea, Italian, whatever, no husband is going to admit to getting another woman pregnant." Rick interjected.

"Trust me, BJ comes from a well-connected family. If they think Jeremy has disrespected her in some way, they'll make him pay." Sandy stated.

"I don't want any more contact between you and the Morganos." Rick was insistent.

"Is that an order?"

"He's right, Sis, stay away from them."

"Paul, where's Erika?" Sandy changed the subject.

"At Renee's. Family business."

"Her father's estate?" Rick asked.

"Among other things which I can't get into." Paul answered.

"If it's about her mother being a lesbian or bi, that's old news.

237

She and Lisa Taylor, the bald-head beauty hair care mogul have been kicking it for years." Macklin chimed in.

"You knew?" Paul was surprised.

"Everyone knew, Paul." Beverly said.

"Everyone except Erika. She's discovered a lot about both her parents and is having a hard time dealing with it." Paul helped himself to some of the food Rick had laid out.

"I'm sorry to hear that, Paul." Beverly joined him at the table.

"So am I, and we need to be supportive. Please let her know we are her friends and we're here for her." Sandy added.

"Thanks. She'll be happy to hear that."

"Me, too, man." Macklin patted Paul on the back. "And I'm sorry, I didn't mean to be so insensitive."

"No problem. And she's still determined to bring Jeremy to justice."

"So, what's the plan, Mr. Cherokee? How do we expose Jeremy's Pub?" Macklin asked.

"We put them on blast. Bev will host a show about what college students who need to work while going to school are subjected to. We'll ask students to call in and share their experiences."

"We'll include a segment on medical issues women face as a result of sexual exploitation; STDs, unwanted pregnancies, mental and physical abuse." Beverly said.

"And not just in the restaurant industry." Mack added. "We all know how the show biz industry takes advantage of young women *and* men."

"Good. Let's do it."

The ratings for the Rick Cherokee show featuring working

college students went through the roof. The phone lines in the control room lit up with students sharing their stories, outraged parents, and sympathetic employers, especially restaurant owners offering jobs to students. The consensus at the end of the show was that there needed to be follow-up shows. Many listeners suggested the students report their exploitation to law enforcement. Some wanted the names and locations of the restaurants so they could be boycotted.

CHAPTER 37

After her conversation with Carl Callahan, Detective Johnson asked Lisa Taylor to come in for an interview.

"Does Mrs. Wallace know you hired a private detective to follow her husband?" Johnson asked.

"Private detective? I don't know what you're talking about." Lisa answered calmly.

"So, you never hired Carl Callahan?"

"Who's Carl Callahan?"

"The private detective you hired."

"Oh, that Carl Callahan."

"Look, Ms. Taylor, I don't have time to play games. I'm investigating the murder of Kenneth Wallace and I think you hired your cousins Lance and Gerard Barrington to kill him."

"I didn't hire Lance or Gerard or anyone else to kill Kenny." Lisa shifted in her chair.

"What about Callahan?"

"I hired Callahan to get evidence to help Renee with the divorce."

"Let me see if I got this straight: you hired Callahan to get evidence that Renee could use in her divorce?"

"Yes."

"You sure about that? You didn't hire Callahan to do anything else?

"No." Lisa knew Johnson didn't believe her, but she wasn't ready to disclose that she had asked Callahan to find her daughter.

"But you did ask the Barrington brothers to take Kenny out." Johnson said.

"I asked Lance to *talk* to Kenny, that's all." Lisa tried to remain calm but was getting nervous. She had the feeling that the detective knew a lot more.

"Lance said you wanted Kenny dead." Lance never said that, but Lisa didn't know that. Maybe he did, maybe he didn't. It's an old interrogation cop trick. Make the perp think you got stuff you don't.

"I only wanted Lance to convince Kenny to give Renee a divorce. Kenny owed Lance a lot of money. If Kenny gave Renee a divorce, the debt would be forgiven. That's all I asked him to do, I swear." Her voice was cracking.

"Well, I guess he must have misunderstood what you meant by *convince*."

"I just wanted Kenny to give Renee a divorce. He didn't give a shit about Renee. He was a pervert, and he was holding my relationship with Renee over her. Besides, he had stolen money from Renee's Hair Care account. At first, he denied it, but then he admitted it and was bragging about how clever he was. He was such a snug bastard."

"So, you did want him dead."

"Not dead, just out of our lives." She was emotional and teary-eyed.

"And now he is."

"But not because of me."

"Who then? Lance, Gerard?"

"Kenny owed Lance money. Why would he kill him? You should be talking to Jeremy Morgano. He was at the restaurant that night trying to shake down Lance."

"How did you know Jeremy Morgano was at the restaurant on the night of the shooting? Were you there?"

"No, I wasn't. Kenny got caught in the crossfire. You know, the wrong place at the wrong time."

"Is that what Lance told you what happened?"

"Yes. Am I free to go?"

"Yes, you are."

Lisa returned to the penthouse after her interview with Detective Johnson.

She fixed herself a drink and called out for Renee.

Renee walked out of Kenny's den. She had found the handwritten note: *'Saw Lisa at Barrington's tonight. Think she and Lance are related – cousins.'*

"Why didn't you tell me Lance Barrington is your cousin?" Renee had a bottle of Vodka in one hand and Kenny's note in the other.

"I was going to." Lisa saw the bottle in Renee's hand and was concerned. Renee had been drinking a lot lately.

"What other nuggets have you been concealing?" She threw Kenny's note at her.

Lisa read the note. "I was going to tell you."

"When! Before or after you had him killed?"

"I don't like the insinuation."

"And I don't like being lied to."

"I never lied to you, Renee."

"I guess lying by omission doesn't count. Did you know Kenny was going to be at Lance's club the night he got shot?"

"No, I didn't, and Lance had nothing to do with Kenny getting shot."

"And you know this how? Is that what cousin Lance told you?"

Lisa drained her glass and poured another. She knew she should have told Renee about Lance, but she was so consumed with getting Kenny out of their lives, it never occurred to her that Renee might *not* want Kenny out of her life.

"According to Lance, Jerry Morgano or one of his friends shot Kenny."

"Who's Jerry Morgano?" Renee asked.

"He and his family own a chain of restaurants. They also supply Cavello wines and liquors to restaurants throughout the state. They've been overcharging Lance and he was threatening to buy elsewhere. Jerry Morgano, wasn't pleased." Lisa explained.

"Okay, but what does any of that have to do with Kenny?"

"Nothing, except Kenny just happened to be sitting in Lance's office when Jerry and his thugs barged in with guns blazing and Kenny got shot."

"Wrong time, wrong place."

"Unfortunately." Lisa nodded.

"Or maybe Lance shot Kenny because Kenny owed him money." Renee said.

"Lance was willing to forgive the debt, if Kenny gave you a divorce."

"And you just assumed I wanted a divorce."

"Well, didn't you?" Lisa was surprised.

"What I wanted was for Kenny to amend our pre-nup and

revise his Will, so I'd get a better percentage of what he's worth. His Will exempts me from the traditional spousal inheritance."

"You never told me that. Now who's keeping secrets?"

"It was none of your business."

"So, what does this mean?"

"It means I won't inherit any of his estate. I wanted him to revise his Will so that I would be entitled to the 1/3 (or more) spousal inheritance. In exchange, I wouldn't tell the SEC about his gambling and that he might have been stealing money from his clients."

"So, you get nothing now?" Lisa asked.

"I'm still the beneficiary on his life insurance policies, but that's small potatoes compared to what I would have gotten from his estate."

"So, Erika gets it all?"

"Yeah, including this penthouse."

"I thought you didn't want it. Plus, you, *we've* got more than enough to buy another one."

"Lisa, I never said I didn't want it. *You* didn't want it because of Kenny. Your resentment of him turned into rage. I had everything under control, but now because of you, Kenny's dead and Erika has control of everything." She took the glass from Lisa's hand. "Get out!"

"What!?

Renee pressed the button for the elevator for the penthouse. "I said get out."

"You're going to regret this, Renee." Lisa stepped onto the elevator.

Renee was upset. She knew Lisa despised Kenny but was she capable of murder? She was trying to decide how she is going to handle this newfound information when the intercom buzzed. Jake the doorman was on way up with a delivery. She wasn't expecting a delivery.

"Good afternoon, Mrs. Wallace." Jake stepped off the penthouse elevator.

"Hello, Jake. What's up? I wasn't expecting a delivery."

"I know, but I need to talk to you." He had a weird look on his face.

"Is everything okay?" Renee asked.

"Mr. Wallace was always kind and respectful to me unlike some of these other folks who live here who confuse doorman with doormat, if you catch my drift."

"Yes, Jake, unfortunately, I do, and I will definitely speak on it at the next board meeting."

"Much appreciated, however, that can wait. Thing is Mrs. Wallace, ever since Mr. Wallace passed on, may he rest in peace, there's been a lot of people nosing around."

"Probably the press. They can be a royal pain."

"Yes, ma'am, I agree; however, it I don't think it's the press. No disrespect intended, but Mr. Wallace's shooting is old news, especially in this town."

"True, however, the police are still investigating."

"Yea, yea, I'm aware of that too, however, this guy is not NYPD, and trust me, I know the po-po when I see 'em."

"Thanks, Jake."

"Sure thing, Ms. Wallace. And don't worry, I'll let you know if I see anything suspicious." Jake took the elevator down to the lobby.

A chill ran down Renee's back. She called her daughter. "We need to talk."

Erika heard the urgency in her mother's voice. Despite their recent estrangement, the mother/daughter bond kicked in. "What's wrong, Mommy? Are you okay?"

"We need to talk, Erika. Are you with Paul?"

"Why?"

"Is he with you, Erika?"

"No."

"Get here as fast as you can."

"What's wrong, Mommy? Erika was alarmed.

"I think I'm being watched."

Ever since Kenny's death, Renee had been having trouble sleeping. She had been drinking more than usual and had started taking sleeping pills. She was also getting calls late at night from people claiming to know who killed her husband. Because she had been drinking and taking pills, she wasn't sure if the calls were real or if she had been dreaming.

She now realized the calls were real and she was being watched. To make matters worse, she now suspected Lisa was responsible for her husband's murder.

Renee was sitting at Kenny's desk when Erika got there.

"Okay, mother, I'm here. What's the problem?"

"Problems." Renee corrected.

"Okay, problems."

"Lisa hired a private eye to look into your father's extramarital affairs."

"Lisa hired a private eye not you?"

"I really didn't need to. I already knew about his infidelity, as well as his addiction to gambling and pornography."

"So why did Lisa hire a PI?"

"Because she wanted me to divorce Kenny."

Erika smirked. "Why, so you two could get married?"

"In a different world, yes. She wanted me free and clear. She hated that Kenny was using our relationship over me. He was the pervert."

"And two women having sex with each other is perfectly acceptable?"

"I realize that many, like you, find our relationship objectionable."

"So, if you knew about daddy's *addictions,* why didn't you divorce him?"

"It wasn't necessary. Your father and I agreed to keep each other's secrets. However, he wasn't the only one keeping secrets. Lance Barrington and Lisa are cousins." Renee showed Erika the note.

"That bitch! Do you think Lisa had something to do with daddy's murder?"

Renee hesitated before answering, then shook her head. "I don't know."

"Did you tell her what you suspected?"

"Yes, I did, and I threw her out. She was mad and said I would regret it.

Lisa Taylor had experienced hardships and heartaches from a young age. Her mother suffered from severe depression and eventually had to be committed to a hospital and her father was killed in Vietnam. Lisa for all intents and purposes was an orphan at age 9. To avoid state intervention, Lisa went to live with her Aunt Mary Barrington and cousins Lance and Gerard.

Lisa had struggled with her sexual identity since adolescence.

She tried hard to fight her attraction to girls and hated the way she was feeling. For a while, she managed to dodge her girlfriends' questions about what boy or boys she wanted to *get with.* However, the peer pressure mounted and she decided to *get with* Charles Andre just to shut them up.

Lisa and Charles *got together,* and she got pregnant.

Aunt Mary told Lisa she could stay with her until the baby was born. After that, she and the baby would have to leave. Aunt Mary contacted Sarah Andre and told her Lisa was pregnant and her son Charles was the father. Lisa gave birth to a baby girl and they moved in with Charles Andre, his mother Sarah and his brother John.

Lisa suffered from post-partum depression, a condition that the Andre family was not equipped to handle. Sarah Andre was concerned. Lisa had little interest in her baby girl. Lisa would leave the Andre apartment and not return for days. When she did return, she smelled of alcohol. Her behavior and appearance became more and more bizarre. Charles threw her out.

Lisa returned a year later with her girlfriend and a clean-shaven head demanding to see her daughter. Charles threw her out again. He petitioned the court and was awarded sole custody of his daughter.

After years of drugging, bed-hopping and living from place to place with female lovers she barely knew, Lisa was tired and realized she would be dead if she didn't get her act together.

Lisa passed Miss Clara's Beauty Parlor almost daily. The shop was located on the street level of a Washington Heights apartment building and was owned by Clara Lee Jackson, a streetwise Black woman from Georgia. It was rumored that she and the landlord, Gaylord Nikos, were lovers.

One day, Lisa entered the shop. Miss Clara figured she wasn't there to have her hair done because she had no hair. However, she could see that Lisa was a troubled young woman. Lisa said she needed a job. She had no experience as a hairdresser, but she could wash hair and sweep the hair off the floor at the end of the day. Lisa was hired. She watched the hairdressers as they worked and often asked questions about hairstyling techniques.

Miss Clara took note of Lisa's interest and asked her if she wanted to be a hair stylist. Lisa said yes, she did. Miss Clara made Lisa an offer: if she stopped using drugs and got her GED, she would train her. Lisa stopped using and got her GED. She became one of Miss Clara's top hair stylists. She also developed a hair growth lotion that didn't damage the hair.

Gerard Barrington passed by Miss Clara's one afternoon and saw Lisa's clean-shaven head shining through the shop window. She had the first chair which was indicative of her status. Gerard rushed home to tell Lance he had seen Lisa working at Miss Clara's. They were now living in an apartment in the Bronx. They both had disagreed with their mother when she told Lisa she and baby could no longer live with them. Lance had been particularly upset. He knew Charles had the baby, but no one knew where Lisa was. Charles said Lisa was a bald-headed, lesbian junkie and he would call the cops if she ever came near *his* daughter.

Lance and Gerard went to Miss Clara's and told Lisa she was coming home with them. Lisa stayed with her cousins for several years. She continued working at Miss Clara's and Lance paid her tuition at The Manhattan School of Beauty.

Lisa developed and patented her hair care products and

started her own line: Lisa Taylor Hair Care, Inc., which she sold to beauty salons, including Miss Clara's.

Clara and Gaylord got married and moved to Greece. Clara sold the shop to Lisa. The shop flourished for years. Everything changed when crack cocaine hit the streets. Even though Lance and Gerard helped with security, the shop was burglarized regularly. Lisa finally had had enough. She sold the shop and used the proceeds to buy an apartment in Brooklyn, where she began selling her hair care products from home.

Lisa called Charles on several occasions asking about her daughter. Charles forbade any contact and threatened to call the police if she tried.

Lisa stopped calling Charles. She knew that when the time was right, she would find her daughter.

CHAPTER 38

They were sitting in Lance's den at his townhouse sipping brandy.

"I'm sorry about you and Renee but can't say I'm surprised." Lance could hear the hurt and sadness in Lisa's voice as she told him about her argument with Renee.

"Really? I never knew you had any bad vibes about Renee."

"Jamaican intuition." He shrugged. "I never thought Renee was being straight, pardon the pun, with you. I think she's been playing you for years."

"Really?" Lisa was surprised at his assessment.

"Yea, really. True, your relationship is as they say, an open secret, but...

"Lance." Lisa interrupted. "The only reason Renee hasn't fully *come out*, is because she was trying to protect Erika."

"Protect her from what--- *you?*"

"Our relationship." Lisa answered. "There are a lot of entanglements."

"Spooky actions at a distance." Lance said.

"What?

"I read somewhere that's how Einstein once described entanglements. Of course, he was referring to physics, but it's appropriate for relationships too."

"Interesting." Lisa nodded.

"And I ain't buying the motherly instinct defense either. Your girlfriend is smart and shrewd, as was her late husband."

"I hired a private detective to gather evidence Renee could use in a divorce proceeding."

"You, not Renee?" Lance was puzzled.

"Yes. Anyway, he found out Kenny was a pervert who liked having sex with underage girls in pigtails, wearing cheerleader outfits." Lisa was accusatory.

"Okay, Kenny was a pervert. Yet, Renee stayed married to him."

"Because he had pictures of us in bed."

"How the hell did he get pictures of you two in bed?"

"Long story short, he had cameras installed in their bedroom."

"You were in *his* bed?" Lance was incredulous. "Cuz, that was just plain dumb."

"I know; I know." Lisa was tired of hearing how dumb it was. "Anyway, because of their pre-nup, Renee gets nothing if she cheated on him. Same thing with his Will."

"So, why didn't *he* divorce her?"

"Because *she* knew he had stolen money from her investment portfolio and threatened to go the SEC if he tried to divorce her."

"So, the kid gets everything?"

"Except for his insurance. Renee is still his beneficiary, although she claims its small potatoes, her words, compared to what his estate is worth."

Lance replenished her glass. "So, what happens now? I mean you're welcome to stay here as long as you need to."

"Thanks, but no. This is just a pit stop. I needed a little TLC." Lance had always been Lisa's refuge in a stormy land.

"Remember the jerk chicken I used to make?"

"Sure do."

"Good, 'cause I got some in the oven and you, me and Gerard, who should be here shortly, gonna have a good ole jerk chicken, with veggies and Rum Lemonade Henny dinner. You down?"

"What you tink?" They high-five.

Gerard Barrington let himself into his brother's house. Gerard was over 6 feet, muscular and handsome. He was wearing a green and black sweat suit with his gym's logo printed down the legs of both sides of his pants and a black baseball cap. Gerard was an ex-professional weightlifter. He made a killing on the professional circuit and now owned two fitness centers.

"Hey cuz, what's up?" Gerard kissed her cheek.

"I'm good, cuz. Love the suit. You're a walking billboard."

"Thanks." He patted her hips. "Um."

"What does 'um' mean?"

"It means JP was right, you haven't been in the gym lately."

Lisa laughed. "JP been telling you my business?"

"That's his job; to keep track of my clientele."

"FYI, I got a lot going on."

"Even more reason to work off some of the tension." Gerard said.

"You right, cuz. I'll be back soon." Lisa poured another drink.

"Police give us the okay to open?" Lance asked his brother. The Barrington had been closed since Vic Russo sprayed the restaurant with bullets and Lance was anxious to reopen.

"Not yet, but it should be soon. They've gone over the place and collected whatever they need." Gerard answered.

"As soon as they're done, get our cleaning guys in there."

"Done. What about the firemen?" Gerard asked. He wanted to torch one of the Morgano restaurants in retaliation.

"Hold up on that. Benny Cavullo called me."

"No shit, Benny Cavullo called you? What did he want?"

"He wants to negotiate. Says we can buy directly from him at a better price."

"And cut out the Morganos?"

"Yep."

"No shit."

Erika tried to allay her mother's fears about being watched.

"It's probably Uncle Robert." Erika knew Robert wanted to talk to his sister and had been waiting across the street from her apartment building hoping to see her.

"He figured, you'd hang up if he tried to call you."

"He was right."

"You should talk to him, Ma. It's been a long time."

"Maybe."

Erika was stunned that her mother had thrown Lisa out of the penthouse. The revelation about Lisa and Lance was equally as alarming. Did Lisa have something to do with her father's death? If so, would she harm Renee if she thought Renee would tell the police?

Erika told Paul about Lisa and Lance Barrington being cousins. She also told him Renee had confronted Lisa and had thrown her out.

"I'm worried Paul. Lisa still has keys. She might try to hurt my mother."

"I don't think Lisa would hurt your mother physically. She loves her."

"People kill people they love."

Erika called her mother. No answer.

"I'm worried. Call a cab. We've got to get to the penthouse."

Renee was sprawled across her bed when Erika and Paul got there. Paul picked up the empty bottle of Vodka on the table near Renee's bed. "This is not good, Erika. And there are pills on the floor."

"Mommy, Mommy!" Erika shook Renee trying to wake her. She got a wet towel from the bathroom and rubbed her forehead. Renee groaned. They got her into the shower. The water revived her.

"I'm alright." Renee shivered. "Get me a robe from the closet. I'm soaking wet."

"You scared me, Ma. Were you trying to kill yourself?" Erika picked up the Vodka bottle. "There are pills on the floor."

"No, I wasn't trying to kill myself."

"Did you let Lisa back in here? She's responsible for this, I know it. First daddy, now you." Erika grabbed a robe from the closet, threw at Renee and left the room.

"Erika!" Paul picked of the robe and handed it to Renee.

"Thanks, Paul. I'm okay. Let me get out of these wet clothes. You take care of Erika." Paul went to the living room.

"This is all Lisa's fault. She's behind this." Erika was pacing.

"Do you really think she had your father killed?" Paul asked.

"She didn't pull the trigger, but she's responsible."

"No, she's not. And like it or not, Lisa and I are lovers, and we were lovers long before I married your father." Renee walked into the living room. She was wearing a bathrobe and her hair was wrapped in a towel turban-style. She sat down on one of the sofas and crossed her legs.

"I'm glad you're okay, Renee." Paul opened a bottle of water. "We were worried."

"Thanks for your concern. I threw Lisa out when I learned she and Lance Barrington are cousins. Maybe I overreacted." Renee said.

"Do you think she had something to do with Kenny's death?" Paul asked.

"It's no secret that she disliked Kenny, but it's hard for me to believe she had anything to do with his death." Renee got up and poured herself a drink.

"I don't think you should be drinking, especially since you took those pills." Paul said.

"Please, those things couldn't knock out a newborn. I haven't been sleeping well so I bought some pills to help me sleep. I was frustrated and threw the bottle in the basket. I missed and some of the pills spilled onto the floor. Everything came down on me and the next thing I knew, I was out like a light."

"What about Lance being Lisa's cousin? Erika asked.

"That was a shock. During this whole police investigation, she never mentioned knowing Lance Barrington, let alone that they're related, but I still don't think she's responsible for your dad's death." Renee said.

"What do the police think?" Paul asked.

"Detective Johnson called me. The bullet that hit daddy was fired by a man named Thomas Russo, who is now dead. His brother Victor Russo was there as well. The police suspect Tommy Russo was killed by a hired gun and Victor was killed by police officers after he shot up the restaurant."

"What restaurant?" Renee asked.

"The Barrington. It was in the papers." Paul answered.

"Although Detective Johnson didn't say it outright, I think there's a connection between the two. However, the bottom line, there's no one to charge for daddy's murder." Erika said.

"Well, in a way justice has been served, the guy who killed your dad is himself dead." Paul observed.

"So, who shot Macklin Hawkins?" Renee asked.

"Victor Russo shot Macklin, and he's dead too."

"Karma's a bitch." Paul said shaking his head.

Erika nodded in agreement, however she wondered if her father's threat of exposing Albert Miller as an embezzler might have something to do with his murder. Could the mild-mannered, always acquiescent Albert Miller have hired a hitman to kill her father?

Rick Cherokee had been careful. He had instructed the students who appeared on the show about working while attending college not to disclose the names of the employers. However, it didn't take long for the students' friends on social media to identify and post the names and addresses of the restaurants, which included Jeremy's Pub, all of which went viral. The blogs and postings were non-stop and unkind. Jeremy's Pub was dubbed Jeremy's Sex Den, a restaurant where old men can order dinner and have sex with young women *and* men.

Business dropped in an internet second.

The legal department of Vantage College issued a statement that the college had no knowledge of what was going on at Jeremy's Pub and the athletic department canceled its scholarship award dinner, as did other colleges. Fraternities, sororities and local businesses also canceled events at Jeremy's.

The Morgano's closed Jeremy's Pub.

✧

As a result of Rick's show, the IRS audited the financial records of the restaurant. They contacted Barbara Jean Morgan who was the secretary/treasurer of Jeremy Morgano, Inc., d/b/a Jeremy's Pub.

After the IRS contacted BJ, she called Erika Wallace. She had found the ledger Jeremy kept regarding the private parties, which included names and dates, as well as monies received. She sent a copy of the ledger to Erika. BJ also gave a copy of the ledger to the IRS agent when she was interviewed. She suspected the income from the private parties had not been reported to the IRS.

The IRS scheduled an interview for Jeremy Morgano. Prior to the interview, Jeremy learned that the agent was a middle-aged man with twin boys, both of whom had applied to Ivy League colleges. Jeremy was reasonably sure it would be a financial strain for him to pay for kids' college education on his government salary. During the course of their first meeting, Jeremy let the agent know he was aware of the agent's impending indebtedness and *suggested* he might be able to help. The agent knew a bribe when he heard one and consulted with his superiors at the IRS, who told him to play along. Although reluctant to wear a wire, he agreed once he was assured detection of the wire would be nearly impossible in the event Jeremy got suspicious.

At the next interview, the agent showed Jeremy the ledger

from the private parties. Jeremy quickly realized that BJ must have turned over the ledger to the IRS. His fuse was burning, but he knew he couldn't do anything to BJ, at least not at the moment. Instead, he offered the agent a bribe which was caught on tape. Jeremy was arrested by the Feds for soliciting a bribe.

In addition, the IRS slapped a fine on Jeremy Morgano, Inc., d/b/a Jeremy's Pub for back taxes to the tune of $6.5 million. The Morgano properties were auctioned off. The Cavullos bought two of the properties, which included Jeremy's Pub for $5,000.

BJ planned to reopen Jeremy's Pub's, under a new name, and staff the restaurant with college students.

She also planned to open a women's health clinic on the other property, and asked Dr. Sandra Hawkins to run the facility.

Barbara Jean Morgano divorced Jeremy.

CHAPTER 39

One Year Later

Reparations Theatre Presents AFTER, by Paul Simmons

> *"AFTER?!"* *What the hell does that mean? After what? After I'm gone; figuratively or literally? After I'm dead? Or is this just more of your philosophical rantings about the evilness of humanity? The corruption of the spirit, bullshit? Or another one of your famous metaphors? What's the matter, the cat suddenly got your tongue? You think this is funny?"*
>
> *"No."*
>
> *"Then why are you laughing""*
>
> *"You're about to find out."* **(GUNSHOT)**

There was a standing ovation as the curtain was lowered. The cast took their bows as Paul thanked everyone, especially his wife Erika, the owner and artistic director of Reparations Theatre. Erika joined Paul on stage and thanked everyone for their support and invited everyone to the after-party.

"The entire cast will there and there'll be lots of food and drink." She kissed her husband.

Renee had tears in her eyes as she blew kisses to her daughter. Lisa was standing next to Renee. They hugged each other. Renee's brother, Robert and his family are also in attendance. Erika had finally convinced her mother to make amends with Robert.

"I am so proud of Erika and she was right, Paul has definitely written a Tony-award winning play." Robert told his sister.

"Yes, those two are definitely going places. Kenny would be proud." Renee kissed her brother's cheek. "Glad you're here, bro."

"You know I couldn't disappoint my favorite niece. Wouldn't have missed it for the world."

Beverly Andre and Macklin Hawkins were also in the front row. Macklin's TV show had been picked up for another season. He and Bev had recently married and were expecting their first child.

Cherokee Media had expanded its network. Rick was planning to propose to Dr. Sandy later that evening.

Elliot Osbourne was on his laptop typing a rave review.

Lisa Taylor approached Beverly. "Ms. Andre, I'm Lisa Taylor and a fan of your show".

"Thanks. Ms. Taylor, you look familiar, have we met? Bev asked.

"Yes, a long time ago."

"A long time ago?" Bev repeated. "That's interesting. I'm a journalist, I deal with when, what and why and I generally don't forget faces."

"Well, like I said, it was a long time ago. However, for reference, I'm Renee Wallace's partner.

"Oh, you're *that* Lisa Taylor." Beverly nodded and winked.

"I get that a lot." Lisa smiled. "However there's much more I'd like to talk with you about at a more convenient time. I'll give you a call." Lisa smiled again and walked back to Renee.

"That's Lisa Taylor, the bald-headed hair growth product mogul." Macklin informed Beverly.

"Yea, I know. She wants to talk to me."

"Probably wants to pitch a show to you."

"Nah. I have a feeling it's something else."

Lance Barrington and his brother were also at the opening. The Barrington had reopened a few weeks after Victor Russo shot up the place. Despite the shootings, business was booming and enjoys the infamous reputation as the place where the rich, famous and notorious meet, eat and drink --- and occasionally get shot.

Lance Barrington tapped Lisa on the shoulder. "Hey Cuz."

"Lance, you made it." Lisa kissed his cheek. Renee, this is my cousin Lance." Renee nodded.

"It's a pleasure to meet you, Renee. I loved the play and the theatre." He sensed the awkwardness of the moment. "I didn't express my condolences to you when Kenny passed and as time passed, I wasn't sure how to. Perhaps, we can have dinner sometime."

Renee nodded and smiled. "Sure. I'd like that."

Renee had reassessed her feelings about a lot of things. She and Lisa were in a good place. She had moved out of the Wallace penthouse and was living in a condo *she* owned. Lisa still had her place in Brooklyn.

Most importantly, Renee and Erika were friends again. Erika had come to terms with her mother and Lisa, as well as her father's character flaws.

The Cavullos, (Benny, his two sons and BJ) were also in attendance. BJ was holding hands with the new man in her life.

BJ walked over to Sandy during the after-party.

"BJ, you look great." Sandy told her. "I'm so glad you made it."

"Thanks, Sandy, you're looking well yourself."

"You know, doc, there's something I've been meaning to ask you."

"Sure, what?"

"What happened to the baby?"

THE END

EPILOGUE

"This is Beverly Andre and I'm happy to introduce Detective Dakota Johnson as our guest today on the Rick Cherokee Show. Our viewers will recall that thanks to the excellent police work of Detective Dakota Johnson, Arturo Morgano and his son William "Billy" Morgano were indicted on several counts of criminal racketeering. It is widely rumored that the mayor will appoint Detective Johnson as the next police commissioner, making her the first Black woman to hold that office."

Printed in the United States
by Baker & Taylor Publisher Services